Tr

Witch

P. G. Allison

Cover Design 2019 by Cormar Covers
www.cormarcovers.com

Tracy the Fire Witch

missy.werecat@verizon.net

To be notified when P. G. Allison's next novel is released, go to:
http://eepurl.com/bCtlh5 and sign up for the Missy the Werecat Newsletter. Your email address will never be shared and you may unsubscribe at any time.

Tracy the Fire Witch

Table of Contents

We actually knew them. They were werewolves. The man was the son of the Beta in the pack which Amanda came from. And, the woman was originally in my pack in Montreal. She was the girl who went to Germany twenty years ago in exchange for Amanda coming to live with my family."

This was a surprise and brought several comments and condolences from those in the room and on the phone. Having the tragic outcome from a WIJO attack affect some of their own personally made it all the more horrific. There was a lengthy discussion. While Gene hadn't known the girl very well and Amanda had barely known the man who died, she had known the man's father quite well because he was a close friend of her father's. The team was interested in finding ways they could help.

Linda Rayburn said, "Hey, if Oliver and Candace are willing to go over there and Gene and Amanda want to go along as well, helping with introductions, then I'd like to go as the "P" Branch support person. I know Les and Marsha will be busy in Kabul, supporting Missy and Mike, so they aren't really available for that."

The team discussed this at length and made a call to Oliver and Candace. When it was confirmed they were definitely interested, a plan began to formulate. The "P" Branch jet was already leaving from Boston on Sunday night, after Robert's wedding, to bring Mike, Les and Marsha to Kabul. It would be an easy stop on the way to drop people off in Berlin. When they needed it, there was a train they could take from Berlin to Munich which only took four hours.

Lieutenant Colonel Schermerhorn said, "I think what's needed for this Germany adventure is a little more firepower. If you want to stir up those terrorists and make them scramble, Oliver's presence might not be enough. I think we should see if Tracy is willing to go along as well. She's on spring break as of today. Let's give her a call."

Tracy and John were halfway home to John's place when Robert's call came in. John was driving but Tracy switched to speakerphone so he could participate in the call as well. Were they interested in helping the team? Spending a week in Berlin? Oh, yes! Tracy had brought her passport with her, as usual, never going anywhere without it. They could be ready to leave Sunday night, right after Robert's wedding. Absolutely!

Robert said, "Colonel Schermerhorn is going to ask Captain Bonomo if he'll go along. He'll be up here for my wedding and we think having him there in Germany with the rest of you might come in handy. We don't know what might come up but, hopefully, this will lead to something. If it does, having someone there with military connections will be good."

"Well, John and I are looking forward to this," said Tracy. "But we're also looking forward to watching you and Connie get married again on Sunday. See you then!" They ended the call. She turned to John and said, "I know I spoke for the two of us but I assume you're okay with these new plans. You are, right?"

"Yeah, I sure am." John glanced at her with a big grin. "As long as I'm able to be with you, twenty-four-seven, then I don't care where we are. Germany?

Werewolves? Maybe some terrorists? What's not to like?" He focused back on his driving and they continued up to his apartment in Easton, just south of Boston.

Chapter One
Saturday, Mar 14, 2020

Tracy McGonagle awoke gradually, aware of being in John's bed rather than her own bed at West Point, aware of being naked rather than wearing the nightgown she typically wore at the academy, and aware of John's warm naked body being closely wrapped around hers. She *loved* being naked. It was naughty, it was sexy and it was fun. Even more than that, she *loved* experiencing John's naked body in such close, intimate contact with hers. Most of all, she *loved* the way John's lovemaking always made her feel so wonderful, in every possible way. Now, fully awake, she stayed right there and allowed herself time to reflect and enjoy thinking about the man she believed was her soulmate.

John McCrea was six feet and had a very nice build. With his handsome features, deep blue eyes, thick reddish brown hair and that winsome smile of his, combined with the wry mischievous expression he always seemed to have ... well, she knew exactly why he had captivated her so much, right from the beginning. And, after all their lovemaking since then, she knew she'd never have eyes for anyone else. She felt very secure about the love they shared for one another. She had no doubt he was her soulmate and, the way her witchy powers had magnified once they'd committed themselves to one another, it was obvious the Fabulous Fates had agreed.

Before they made love, there was the anticipation. Always exciting, always such a thrill. She never would know exactly what they might do but she could always be sure whatever they did, it would be great. During their lovemaking, there were no words adequate for the experience; she and John would become one in mind, body and soul. And after? Her sated, satisfied essence would soar. Sometimes, she would then fall asleep and that essence of hers would freely find its way through whatever fantasies awaited her while she dreamed. Other times, her feeling so fulfilled would result in her drawing energy from all around, immediately replenishing whatever had been expended such that she was more awake and alive than ever. Ahh, the wonders of being a witch!

She slipped out of bed without waking John up and used the bathroom. Then, she crept back into bed and began rubbing her now cold breasts up against John's warm back ... her *pretty, perky, perfect* breasts according to John, who loved to exaggerate and, though he was certainly biased, nonetheless was always praising them. She had actually stopped wishing they were bigger, thanks to all his words of admiration. And, of course, thanks to all the attention he typically gave them which left no doubt as to how he felt about them. Today she and John were not in any hurry and planned only on enjoying one another. So, she wanted them to leisurely start enjoying one another right now. Right away. Right?

John had actually snuck out of bed earlier, using the bathroom and returning before Tracy had gotten up. He'd been aware of her every movement and, when she'd returned to bed as he'd hoped, he felt his clandestine actions had been well rewarded by the way she was behaving now. He loved teasing her so he said, "Hey, what did you do with my girlfriend? You better be careful … she can be a real witch sometimes!"

Tracy chuckled and said, "You mean that poor, shriveled up old hag I found sleeping with you in here earlier? Obviously, she bewitched you into thinking she was your girlfriend, just so she could have her way with you."

John laughed and rolled over so he was on his back, pulled her onto his chest and then ran his hands down to grab and hold her ass. "Gosh, the things she had me doing last night! Why, I was worried the sex police were going to show up and arrest me any minute."

"The *sex* police?" Tracy loved the way he always surprised her with silly stuff like that. "Was your concern perhaps due to any *performance* issues? I understand they have pills you can take …"

"Oh, no! Just the opposite. In fact … I'm not all that surprised you found her shriveled up and looking worn out." John was getting very aroused by the way Tracy had kept wriggling while he was holding onto that lovely rear of hers. "Especially that last thing she had me do with my thing." He shifted his position so his erection had a bit more room and so she would definitely be feeling it throbbing against her lower abdomen.

"Your *thing*? Would that be the very same *thing* which I'm sort of noticing right now?" She grabbed his shoulders and pulled herself upward while grinding her pelvis so he was positioned exactly where she wanted him. "Why don't you do that thing with your thing right now so I can know exactly what … oh!" John had suddenly lifted her up and then pulled her back down, impaling her. She was so wet, he slipped inside easily and she began grinding her pelvis in earnest. That felt so, so good!

The conversation was over and for the next several minutes, there were only moans and groans as they continued making love. Tracy had just started her second orgasm when John finally shuddered, finding his release and emptying inside her. That heightened her enjoyment and she yelled and hollered as her pleasure overwhelmed her completely. For several minutes afterward, they both simply lay there, blissfully clinging together as their bodies relaxed and their soaring souls somehow found their way back into their bodies once again.

Finally, John said, "Wow! And, I thought that thing we did last night was good."

"Yeah, that thing we just did right now was definitely fantastic," agreed Tracy. "MmmMmm. Can we do that again?" The enthusiasm in her voice was unmistakable.

John laughed and, with an exaggerated sigh, said, "Well, not for a while, I'm afraid. I'm sure you've noticed my *thing* has shriveled up and would indeed have some performance issues at the moment."

Tracy giggled and said, "My girly bits are a bit sore, at the moment, so that's quite all right. What shall we do while we give your thing and my bits some time to recuperate?" She hopped out of bed and watched as he got up also.

"First, we eat a nice breakfast," answered John. "Then, we'll drive into Boston, park the car and spend some time cruising through Quincy Market. I haven't taken you there yet and until you visit Faneuil Hall and see why it's called the Cradle of Liberty of the Revolution, why ... you just can't fully appreciate American history."

"Okay, okay. Sounds fun." Tracy had heard about where the Boston Tea Party rebellion against British Taxation had begun and was also aware there were over a hundred shops, pushcarts, restaurants and pubs at this marketplace where Boston's famous Freedom Trail began. "You can drag me around and show me the sights as long as you promise to also feed me lots of good food, give me plenty of chocolate, maybe get me some ice cream and then, bring me back here to ... you know ... satiate *all* of my bodily needs."

"Oh, my plans for your luscious body are all inclusive," laughed John. He had fallen for her immediately, love at first sight, more than a year earlier. She had dark brown hair worn in a nice page boy style, appropriate for an Army cadet. With her naturally lovely complexion, her dark brown eyes always shining brightly and her really pretty smile, she didn't need much else.

15

Although not a great athlete like his sister Missy was, Tracy was very athletic nonetheless, and at five-six with a nice figure, she certainly looked good. As far as he was concerned, she was the most attractive person he'd ever met. The fact that their feelings for one another were mutual had only made him love her all the more.

An hour later they were dressed, had eaten and were on their way to Boston.

When they returned to John's apartment, it was late in the evening. They had done a lot of walking, a lot of talking, a lot of eating and it had all been good. The historic sites had been fascinating. Then, Tracy had been especially thrilled with the Ghirardelli Chocolate and Ice Cream Shop. Plus, she even got to do some last minute shopping for the wedding they were attending the next day as well as for their upcoming Germany trip.

There was some mail waiting and when John looked at what had arrived that day, he got very excited. He quickly tore open one of the envelopes and then said, "Hey, you know that accelerated two-year law degree program I told you I applied for at the New York Law School? I've been accepted!"

"Really? That's wonderful," said Tracy. She rushed over and gave him a big hug. "I know how much you've been counting on that." He was graduating with his bachelor's degree in May and now, assuming he could pass the bar exam two years later, he'd be finishing right when she was graduating from West

Point. Plus, he'd be down in New York City for those two years, much closer to the academy.

John said, "Obviously, those Fabulous Fates you and my sister always talk about are showing us some favor. I'll be ready to follow wherever you go." He knew she had her heart set on going to Fort Rucker, Alabama for the Army Aviation school. She believed it was her destiny to fly attack helicopters so she then could shoot whatever armaments might be appropriate in support of the U.S. troops and her country. She was a fire witch, after all, and had been gifted with the ability to bring down lightning bolts and fireballs. Hence, she felt it was her calling. He had no doubt she would succeed.

She was his girlfriend, his soulmate, and he considered it his destiny to support her wherever she went in whatever she did. It scared the hell out of him that she was a warrior witch but, that's what she was and that's who he'd fallen in love with.

"Yes, that's very true and it will be wonderful," Tracy acknowledged. "Both about our being favored by the Fates and that you'll be able to go wherever I might go. Even if I don't get into flight school right away ..."

"Oh, you will, you will! I don't doubt that at all, Tracy. And, if you need any assistance getting whatever assignments you want? Well, you've got all those friends in high places now whom you've helped already. I mean ... this trip we're taking to Germany is another example. Your government buddies won't let you down after the way you always step up whenever they need you."

"I suppose. Only, I view it differently. They've merely been giving me some opportunities to fulfill my destiny. Aren't you the one who always says a witch has gotta do what a witch has gotta do?" Tracy giggled.

"Well … actually, I'm the one who's going to help fulfill your destiny for the rest of this evening," laughed John. "I see some really hot sex in your immediate future." He began taking off some of his clothes and then approached her with the obvious intent of taking off some of her clothing as well.

"Oh, really? I must admit, I do like the sound of that." She began unbuttoning her blouse and then let him help her with getting undressed.

"Are your tender, sensitive lady bits still sore?" asked John. "If so, then I'll be very gentle. You know how I can be really, *really* gentle when I use my tongue."

Tracy loved it when he was really, really gentle. Until he wasn't. Then, of course, she loved it even more …

Chapter Two
Sunday, Mar 15, 2020

The wedding was a wonderful event. Robert and Connie kept telling everyone it was even better than their first time down the aisle. The reception was held at a Marriott Hotel in Peabody and was well attended. In addition to everyone on his Psychic Division team being there, there were many from other FBI groups who had worked with Robert over the years.

Drew Martinson, Les and Marsha Gooding, Linda Rayburn and two other "P" Branch members were seated at the same table with Lieutenant Colonel Schermerhorn and Captain Bonomo. The captain actually ended up sitting next to Linda which seemed appropriate as they both were single and similar ages, in their mid-twenties. They were pleasantly surprised when they each learned the other would be on the "P" Branch jet to Germany that night and soon found they had a lot to talk about.

Millicent Pratt had come up from Texas. She had been Tracy's mentor and then, at Tracy's request, she had gone to Cancun with Robert and Oliver when Candace had gone missing. She sat with Desiree Yerger who had brought her daughter Delilah. Lila quickly paired up with Missy's brother Patrick and the two of them were off in their own little world, oblivious to everything going on around them. Also at that table were Oliver Bessom with Candace Axtell plus Troy Dangelmeyer with Sally Navarro.

Missy and Mike were at the McCrea table with Missy's parents, Philip and Julia. So was her sister Heather with her husband Donald Whalen plus her brother John with Tracy. Robert had gotten very close to everyone in Missy's family during her two-year disappearance in the mountains.

There were several toasts to the bride and groom all during the delicious meal and then there was dancing. All too soon, the day of celebration came to an end and it was time for Robert and Connie to say goodbye and head off on their honeymoon. They were booked on an early morning fight to Aruba. Everyone cheered when they made their exit from the reception.

Once they had departed, many others also left. Missy went with Mike and the group who were leaving that night on the "P" Branch jet. Sergeant First Class Town was already waiting on board and looking forward to rejoining Team Twenty-Two for the next week. He, Mike, Les and Marsha would continue over to Kabul after dropping the others in Berlin. Missy would be teleporting, of course, so she would reach Afghanistan in only two hours. The Germany group consisted of Gene, Amanda, Oliver, Candy, John, Tracy, Linda and Captain Jesse Bonomo.

Missy waited until the jet took off from Logan Airport and then, wishing the others good luck and kissing Mike goodbye, she disappeared in a shimmer of light and was gone. Marsha went over and picked up all the clothes Missy had left behind.

Linda was very impressed and said, "Wow! I hadn't actually seen her do that before. Seeing is believing!"

Monday, Mar 16, 2020

During the "P" Branch flight to Berlin, which took just over eight hours, everyone tried to grab a few hours of sleep. With the time difference, their arrival was just before noon local time. Of course, there had been some lively discussions prior to anyone nodding off.

First, of course, they'd talked about the wedding they'd just attended. Then Linda and Captain Bonomo wanted to know the details concerning when Candy had been kidnapped. Gene and Amanda were also interested in that story along with how she'd been rescued just prior to her scheduled beheading. Sergeant Town was quite entertaining with his description of Tracy's role in that rescue. He'd explained how watching her set fire to the village perimeter as a diversion had been his introduction to supernaturals. Marsha then reminded everyone they needed to be well rested for the days ahead so they all quieted down and drifted off to sleep.

The flight was uneventful and, after dropping off the Germany group, the jet was back in the air and headed on to Kabul. The group was met right at the airport by Candace's new security team which had come up from the Army Garrison in Ansbach. Since her regular team back in the U.S. had remained behind, General Blake had arranged for this team to provide security for his niece during her stay in Germany. They provided transportation for everyone over to a secure facility which had been assigned for their use inside the old Clay Headquarters Compound in Berlin's Zehlendorf district.

After the U.S. Army's command in Berlin was inactivated in 1994, its housing areas, schools, and various other facilities all reverted to civilian use. Some were for German citizens while others were taken over by the U.S. Embassy. When the new Pariser Platz building for the embassy opened in 2008, it was not large enough and parking was limited at that site. Thus, the Clay Atlee building had continued to be used and the Army still had housing nearby which it could utilize for VIP's, when needed.

Of course, arrangements for Candace and her group had been made very quickly and when they arrived, there was a glitch. Only four rooms had been made available and, due to all the security requirements, finding another room would be difficult.

First Lieutenant Saunders, the officer-in-charge of the security team, told them, "All of the rooms are set up with two double beds in each. We knew there would be four men and four women in your group and hoped this arrangement would be adequate."

Tracy said, "Unfortunately, there are three couples in our group and each couple will want their own room. When John and I agreed to this trip, we definitely were counting on staying together the whole time."

Captain Bonomo offered to bunk wherever the security team guys were staying but, unfortunately, that wasn't a practical solution. After a brief discussion, it was clear there were complications with that as well as some security concerns.

Linda had gotten to know the captain quite well during the many hours they'd now been together and was not at all averse to possibly sharing her room with him. She said, "Well then ... in the interest of keeping things simple and due to security and all ..." She looked with raised eyebrows over to see what Captain Bonomo might say to what she was now proposing. "Maybe Jesse can stay with me. Since there are two beds in the room, it really shouldn't be a problem."

Jesse was finding her more and more attractive and, realizing what she was offering, he was quick to reply. "This would of course be strictly platonic, but yeah! If that's really okay, then sure. Simple. Secure." He smiled warmly at Linda and then looked around at the others.

Tracy had been noticing the way the two of them had been getting quite comfortable with each other and thought this was indeed an excellent solution. "Great! Problem solved. Let's all drop off our bags and then we can maybe go over to the embassy for a quick tour. Right?" She would tell John later how she was convinced those Fabulous Fates may have once again allowed Cupid to shoot a few of his arrows. Yes, it was going to be an interesting week!

Gene said, "Good idea. Amanda and I served years ago with Felicity Miller. She's been assigned here for the past two years now. When we emailed her about this earlier and mentioned how General Blake has been having his niece visit embassies, she agreed to be our host. I'll let her know we're on our way."

When they arrived at the embassy, Felicity was waiting with several others. She greeted them warmly and made the introductions. Looking at Amanda, she asked her, "How does it feel to be here in Germany again?" While not aware Amanda was a werewolf, she did know some of Amanda's history.

Amanda had not been back since her family had sent her away to Canada when she was thirteen. Once females in a werewolf pack demonstrated they were able to Shift, it was common for them to be exchanged to other packs. Arranged marriages were the norm. Being a werewolf was a rare genetic thing, so packs were always concerned about breeding. The best chance for giving birth to more werewolves was when both parents were werewolves. Even then, it was only fifty-fifty.

She was very excited now to once again be returning home. She had kept in touch with her family, even after the disgrace which her mating with Gene and being expelled by his pack had caused. She had moved in with his family and was supposed to mate with his brother Dylan, the Alpha's oldest son. She had no regrets about hooking up with Gene instead, however. Gene was her true soulmate and she looked forward with pride to finally introducing him to everyone here in Germany. She smiled and answered, "I am thrilled about this opportunity to finally return home. Gene and I are very happy we were asked to accompany Candace and her fiancé on this tour."

"Well, good. Let's get started then," said Felicity. "Today will merely be an informal tour, as you've requested, with the formal visit and tour to be on Wednesday." She and the other staff members then led the group out of the Visitor's Center. For the next three hours, they got to see all the key points of interest, visit various offices and meet with members from several other U.S. Government agencies working out of the embassy as well. Candace was quite a celebrity now and, once word got out she was there, everyone wanted to see her.

Tracy and Oliver both checked for other supernaturals but did not notice anyone. Oliver's ability enabled him to sense any residual energy which might remain had any supernatural been present in the recent past, but he didn't notice that either.

At the end of the day, Candace had an opportunity to address everyone interested in hearing from her in one of the large auditoriums. She had spoken about being kidnapped and then sold to WIJO at her other embassy visits and had earned the respect and admiration of many. She had a reputation for being not only beautiful and exciting to see but inspiring to hear as well. There was a huge turnout and it was therefore quite late when the group finally relaxed for dinner in the VIP dining room.

Felicity had arranged for them to dine with a dozen other staffers and, once everyone was seated, she stood and raised her wine glass in a toast. "I want to thank Candace Axtell for visiting us today. The story she told us about her ordeal when WIJO was holding her captive was inspirational. Not many of us could have survived what she did and then been able to confront her enemies afterward as she has been doing." Everyone cheered and then sipped their drinks.

Gene stood to say a few words. "My wife and I served in the foreign service for more than ten years. When Candace visited our embassy in Kabul last Thanksgiving, we learned how important it was to stand up against WIJO the way she is doing. Her presence makes a clear statement against them. The recent bombing attack in Munich was the act of cowards, killing innocent civilians. Candace's presence here is to again make that statement, showing WIJO can be defeated and their acts of terrorism will not succeed." Again, everyone cheered. Then, dinner was served.

Later, when Tracy and John finally were alone in their room, having been escorted back by the security team without incident, John said, "I'm sure word will get out that Candace is here. That speech she gave was wonderful. Do you think any WIJO teams in this country will make any attempts to grab her or kill her?"

"No, I doubt that. From all the Intel which Robert's team has managed to collect since Missy infected so many of the WIJO leaders' computers, they're very determined to *not* fail going after Candace yet again. Their original attempt backfired when we rescued her and, when they failed again in Pakistan, that only embarrassed them even worse. They aren't likely to approve anything their local teams over here might want to try. But, if they do approve sending anyone to go after her during the brief time we're here, Robert's team should hear something. We can get ready if that happens."

The Missy virus software, which Lisa and Marie had created and Missy had installed while in her spirit form, had indeed provided Robert's team with a huge advantage. It enabled remote access to each computer, was not detectable, and allowed the team to review hundreds of communications between the WIJO leaders. Some of those had allowed them to make timely interventions, thwarting WIJO attacks.

John said, "Well, good. We can relax then for now, right? How about you and I getting naked and seeing how quickly we can eliminate all thoughts about WIJO from interfering with how *relaxed* we can get?" He knew how she loved getting naked.

Tracy giggled and, not surprisingly, they both managed to completely forget all about WIJO in no time at all. Their success was such that neither one had a single thought about WIJO for the remainder of the night. Eventually, they even managed to get some asleep.

27

Chapter Three
Mar 16, 2020

Linda had gone up to her room alone since Jesse had graciously agreed to give her time to use their bathroom and get ready for bed while he and Lieutenant Saunders bonded over a beer in the bar downstairs. She was surprised at how her impromptu decision to share her room with him was now affecting her. At the time, it had seemed logical. But, once she'd actually climbed into bed, wearing a modest nightgown which thankfully she'd brought along, she began experiencing butterflies. What had she been thinking? This guy she hardly knew, this *attractive* guy … he would soon be coming up. Then, they'd be alone … together.

When Captain Bonomo did gently knock and then open the door, she was still unsure of how she felt. But, he smiled disarmingly at her and said, "Hey, Linda. I see I gave you enough time. Thanks again for agreeing to share this room with me."

"Well, it was obvious they all wanted their own rooms." Linda smiled and added, "Did you see the expression on Tracy's face when that lieutenant seemed to be suggesting she and John be in *separate* rooms?"

Jesse chuckled and said, "Oh, yes! That was *never* going to happen. Nor was splitting up Oliver and Candace or the Tremblays."

Linda was still trying to find things they could talk about to keep the mood light and easy. No, she wasn't going to allow any sexual tension to creep into the room. She said, "Sooo ... this Tracy is a fire witch. The way that sergeant explained how shocked he'd been at her creating all those fireballs when they'd rescued Candy? He was hilarious."

"Actually, I got to watch when she brought down some lightning bolts. She hit this huge tree outside an estate in Bogota. Three strikes and that tree went down in flames. That was spectacular. Quite a demonstration. Which, of course, was exactly what her friend Missy had wanted. And, it worked. Manuel Rodriguez was convinced Missy was a demon and willingly surrendered."

"Yes, I read about that. "P" Branch still has him tucked away in their prison. You were down there for that?" Linda was impressed.

"I'll never forget it." Jesse sat down on his bed where he could chat with her more easily.

Linda said, "I've never actually met any witches before this weekend. I read all about them in those briefings from "P" Branch but ... I guess I thought they'd be more different somehow. They seem so *normal*."

Jesse grinned. "Well, I've never actually met any werewolves before this weekend. The Tremblays seem pretty normal as well."

"Yes, they are. I guess it's not until you get past that superficial shell all werewolves maintain around their personal lives. They keep their secrets really well. It was only after I'd been dating one for over a year that I found out what he was."

Jesse knew from what Gene had told him that she'd been in a relationship with the Beta of the New England werewolf pack for a couple of years. "P" Branch had recruited her after she'd broken up with him. They continued discussing witches and werewolves for quite a while. And, as they shared how they each had gotten to know all about supernaturals, they got to know more and more about one another.

Finally, Jesse said, "It's probably a good idea for us to get some sleep. We have a big week coming up. I'll just go undress in the bathroom. I hope you don't mind that I sleep in my underwear and don't have any pajamas. Go ahead and turn off the lights and I'll leave the bathroom light on when I come out so it's not totally dark in here."

When he did exit the bathroom and quietly slipped into bed a few minutes later, she was lying with her back facing his bed. She had her eyes closed but was very, *very* aware of his presence none the less. She remained awake and aware long after his heavy breathing suggested he'd fallen asleep. No, she wasn't experiencing any sexual tension. Well, maybe a little …

Jesse did not actually fall asleep right away either, in spite of the way his breathing may have convinced Linda that he had. No, he was finding his thoughts and feelings about the woman in the next bed were keeping him wide awake. It had been a long time since he'd been in a relationship with anyone. And, there were so many things about Linda that seemed to stimulate his senses. Thus, it was much, much later that he did manage to drift off. And then? He dreamed about her all night long.

When Talib Mansoor heard from his source in the American Embassy that Candace Axtell and her demon protector Oliver Bessom had been there that day, he was quite concerned. This was very bad news. He had no choice but to immediately report this back to Mullah Ahmed Kahtar, one of WIJO's top leaders in Afghanistan and his immediate supervisor. His mission in Germany was suddenly at risk.

He'd seen the warnings which the leaders had sent out. He knew Bessom had somehow been responsible for many of WIJO's recent failures and what a disaster it had been each time they'd tried to kill or capture the Axtell girl. Now that his team had successfully bombed that nightclub in Munich? The presence of these two could not be any coincidence. No, all his careful planning for further bombings must wait. He'd notified everyone to assemble at his warehouse right away. That night. He knew he would be hearing back from Mullah with special instructions.

As each member of his team arrived, he explained what had happened and why he had called them in. When they were all gathered in the large meeting room at the warehouse which was also used for his beer, wine and liquor distribution business, he called then all to order.

"Attention everyone." He looked at each of the fourteen men on his team. "I have just learned the Infidel whore Candace Axtell is here and has brought one of the U.S. demons with her. This demon was last seen in England two weeks ago when our attack in London was stopped and Abdullah Jawara was arrested. So was his entire team. I have sent word to Mullah Ahmed Kahtar and we will wait here to learn what our leaders will want us to do."

One of his men asked, "Why must we wait? Surely it will be Allah's will that we destroy these abominations!" There was some murmuring around the room indicating many of them agreed. They all knew what an embarrassment it had been when Candace Axtell had been rescued rather than beheaded. It had been rumored an entire village in Afghanistan had been destroyed.

Mansoor was quick to reply. "We must wait to learn what our leaders say. They have made it very clear there will be no more public failures to disgrace our cause. And, none of us here knows how to defeat the demons which the U.S. is using against us. They are not human. And, they possess great powers. Powers and abilities which we do not yet understand."

Another voice asked, "Will they be investigating what we did in Munich? We left no evidence they can find to trace back to us."

"Who knows what demons can determine? Or, what they can use to search for us? That has been the problem for all our teams which have failed. We must

32

wait for orders. And, if those orders say we must leave Germany, then we will obey."

Mullah Ahmed Kahtar was also concerned when he received Mansoor's report. Askar-Samar Karimi had said the U.S. demons would interfere if there were further WIJO attacks. And, now Bessom was in Germany. Attempts to kill him or Candace Axtell had all failed. Even their surveillance teams had failed. Bessom had chased them away with fireballs.

Mansoor's team would not be successful in either of these efforts and should probably be pulled out. He began calling the other leaders. Karimi was the first one to get his call and that was his recommendation. But Kahtar thought perhaps they could wait a day or so to see what developed. WIJO had invested a great deal in establishing Mansoor in Germany.

Chapter Four
Tuesday, Mar 17, 2020

As arranged, everyone had come down for breakfast at eight. For today's agenda, Oliver, Candy, Jesse and Linda would travel by express train to Munich with only Lieutenant Saunders from the security team on board. However, there would be additional security force members at each stop and at their destination.

John, Tracy, Gene and Amanda would also take the same train but would be traveling separately. The initial visit to the werewolves in Regensburg would be just the four of them while Oliver and the Army team made a big show of investigating the bombing site.

Regensburg was where most of Amanda's pack lived. It had a population of a hundred and fifty thousand, was about an hour and fifteen minutes north of Munich and an hour and a half west of the Bavarian Forest. Amanda's parents were meeting the train in Munich and she was very excited.

Once they were well underway on the Inter-City Express (or ICE train), with the city of Berlin falling quickly behind and their speed approaching two hundred miles per hour, John looked around and said, "Wow. This is pretty impressive." They were in first class, thanks to "P" Branch, and had their own compartment for the four of them equipped with plush armchairs and accessories. There was also a luxurious dining car they could use. "When Tracy told me we were being thrown to the wolves, I had no idea what a wonderful adventure this would be!"

Tracy groaned, looked at Gene and Amanda with exasperation and said, "Please ignore him. His attempt at humor, as usual, is totally inappropriate."

"Actually," smiled Amanda, "his comment probably *is* appropriate. While I'm excited about seeing my family, I can't say Gene and I will be getting greeted with open arms by the rest of the pack."

"Because you mated with Gene rather than his brother?"

"Yes, that … and because we then became rogue wolves, with no pack. Plus, we haven't been breeding yet." Amanda grimaced. "I'm supposed to be increasing the werewolf population, if possible. So, I haven't exactly been fulfilling my destiny. At least … not the destiny my pack's Alpha had in mind when he arranged for me to be exchanged."

Gene said, "And now Justine, the girl who my pack exchanged for Amanda? She won't be breeding any werewolves because she was killed in that bombing. I don't know what the reason may have been, but she and Johan Gerhard never had any children."

"Well, setting aside the tragedy of this terrorist bombing," said Tracy, "I guess I'm finding it difficult to understand this whole destiny business." She glanced at John briefly and then asked, "What about true love and finding your soulmate?"

John said, "Yeah, your pack should be proud of you and Gene. And, you're still young. Are you hoping to have children someday?" He saw Tracy was not happy about his blunt question but, hey … if increasing the werewolf population was such a huge issue?

Amanda noticed Tracy being annoyed with John and rushed to say, "Yes, we would *love* to have children. Until now, we needed to wait. Being in the foreign service, moving around the way we were, and not being in any pack? We just couldn't risk starting a family."

Gene smiled and said, "But, thanks to our new jobs on Robert's team and *especially* now that we're members of the New England pack, thanks to Missy … well, we're actually hoping we can finally start. A family. Hopefully, our children will be werewolves. But, if not, we'll still be happy. Our destiny will have been fulfilled, either way. We don't care what Amanda's former pack might want. Or, my former pack either."

"Congratulations on making that decision," said Tracy. "And, we wish you all the luck in the world. May all your dreams come true!" She looked at John and said, "Maybe my tactless, inappropriately behaving boyfriend and I might someday fulfill our dreams as well. Assuming I decide to forgive him, of course."

John grinned and said, "What happened to our being *soulmates*? Now, I'm merely your *boyfriend*? Woe is me, woe is me!" Everyone laughed at this.

They continued to talk about soulmates, werewolf packs and family for the remainder of their trip, only leaving the privacy of their compartment towards the end so they could enjoy a nice meal in the dining car. When they finally arrived in Munich, they had formed a nice friendship which they knew would be a lasting one.

Oliver and Candace's arrival at the nightclub where the bombing had occurred five nights earlier was purposely ostentatious with a great deal of fanfare. The media had been alerted and, in spite of the short notice, they were quite happy to take photos and videos for the news and showed up in force. The German people had all watched the previous September when Candace had been dragged before the cameras by WIJO. Her last minute rescue had been a big story. And, now she was there in Munich, showing sympathy for those who had been brutally killed by the same WIJO terrorist organization which had wanted to kill her.

The nightclub was closed and marked off with police tape as a crime scene. But the forensic work and other investigative efforts had been completed so Oliver and Candace were allowed to enter and examine the aftermath. The bomb had been hidden inside a backpack which, in spite of tight security, had somehow been smuggled inside and left under a table near one of the support columns. It had then been detonated by a cell phone signal. In addition to the shrapnel from the devastating blast, there had been a great deal of secondary damage with partial collapse of the roof. Fortunately, there had been no fire afterwards as the sprinkler system had activated. Nonetheless, there was debris everywhere and those in proximity to the bomb had suffered injury or death right away.

The fact that Candace was strikingly beautiful with blond hair, deep blue eyes and a smile which would light up any location certainly added to how well she and her entourage were received. It was no surprise she was surrounded by military guards. The presence of so many from the media then drew large crowds and her visit quickly became a big event. When she was asked to say a few words, she was happy to do so. An interpreter was provided and, after another brilliant performance on her part, she was asked many follow-up questions.

Oliver was very visible at her side and she proudly introduced him as her fiancé. The Army guards did an excellent job of protecting them while Linda and Jesse remained in the background. Linda said, "Now I understand why Marsha Gooding suggested this visit as a way to keep WIJO on the defensive and interfere with whatever plans they might have. This will clearly be the top story on all the news channels and far outweighs any statement made by those terrorists."

"Yes," agreed Jesse. "They cannot ignore all this publicity against them and, since Oliver and Missy made themselves visible as demons when they stopped that attack in London, I'm sure Robert's team will be picking up some Intel concerning WIJO's reaction to this. Having Oliver here fulfils the promise Missy made to Karimi that actions would be taken against them if there were further attacks. They won't know what those demon actions might be, of course, and that has to be concerning them now."

"That's the real benefit, isn't it?" chuckled Linda. "That whole *demon lore* business which Colonel Schermerhorn talks about. Fear of the unknown can be very debilitating. From the feedback Robert's team has gotten so far, it's been very effective. Those WIJO leaders don't know what to do about our demons."

"Let's hope their worry about what Oliver might be doing here will lead to their making some mistakes. Then the promise you heard Candace make to the German people just now for justice will become a reality. While Oliver isn't really that much of a warrior witch, we've brought along Tracy. They don't actually know about her but they'll soon learn what justice means if she gets unleashed on them."

Amanda's parents were overjoyed at seeing their daughter get off the train. She had two older brothers who were also there, along with their wives and children. The exuberant greetings as she hugged and kissed each of them were heartwarming. Then the pride and love she exhibited as she introduced each of them to Gene were very obvious. John and Tracy stood by and enjoyed the show and didn't need any translator. It was a truly wonderful family reunion and they were very touched by it.

They soon piled into several vehicles for the ride out to the family home where a large celebration was waiting. During the trip, Amanda translated what her father was explaining. Yes, there were many pack members who were not happy about the disgrace which Amanda had brought on them but, that didn't matter.

They were pack and had gathered together to celebrate her visit regardless.

John asked, "Does everyone know you're bringing a couple of outsiders who are not werewolves?" He knew how secretive witches were and had heard werewolves were even more so.

Amanda and her parents exchanged some quick sentences and then Amanda smiled at John. "Yes, my father has told them how you are bringing your soulmate, who happens to be a witch. They're not thrilled about that but they do understand. Mates are family and can be trusted. So, you both are allowed to visit."

"And, I'm guessing they'll trust John since his sister is the Alpha of the pack you and Gene have just joined, right?" asked Tracy. "Lucky me, having such an esteemed boyfriend … err, soulmate!" She grinned at John.

There was some more discussion in German. Although Amanda's parents both understood English, and knew what Tracy had said, they wanted to share their thoughts with their daughter and then let her translate. Finally, Amanda turned to Gene, Tracy and John and said, "They heard about Missy defeating Brody Billiscombe to take over the New England Pack a couple days before hearing from me about our joining that pack. They actually didn't know until my telling them just now that Missy did that in our behalf. They're very impressed. There haven't been very many female Alphas and there have never been any werecats doing this before. The whole werewolf world has taken this news as quite an extraordinary thing."

John nodded and said, "Ah, well … there are those in this world who are extraordinary and destined for greatness. Then, there are those of us fortunate enough to be mated to such amazing supernatural beings." He pulled Tracy in close and hugged her tightly.

Gene then pulled Amanda over for a big hug and said, "That is so true, John!" The rest of the trip went extremely well with Tracy and Amanda both glowing at being given such praise and affection by their respective mates.

Chapter Five
Mar 17, 2020

Klauss Jäger, the Alpha of the Regensburg pack, was present at the family celebration in Amanda's honor but was not there to give his blessing. He had agreed to come since Hans Gerhard, his Beta and best friend, had asked that he be there. Hans was mourning the loss of his son and daughter-in-law, as was the rest of the pack, and Klauss had come to pay his respects where so many pack members would be gathering.

While he had been very upset about the disgrace which Amanda had caused to his pack years ago, he understood the need for him now to show his acceptance. It was a time for the pack to focus on healing. Thus, he was determined to make peace without any recriminations. He was there. However, he would not be giving any blessings to the visitors.

Amanda listened to her parents' explanation of how the pack had agreed to assemble and would allow her to visit but that it would be more in honor of Jonah and Justine Gerhard. She then translated all this to the others. As she had indicated on the train, while many would greet them warmly, there would be many more who would merely tolerate their presence. She cautioned them not to take offense at this.

There were almost fifty members in the pack and most had come to this gathering which was held in the large hall where the pack typically had its meetings.

They formed several different groups as they waited for Amanda's family to bring the visitors around to be introduced. With Amanda's family guiding them, Gene and Amanda along with John and Tracy slowly worked their way from group to group.

The first group were close friends of Amanda's family and they were very gracious in their welcome. There was much oohing and aahing about how much Amanda had changed from the little girl who had left them all those years ago. Amanda remembered them quite well and thanked them for the friendship and support they'd continued to give her family during the years she'd been away.

Next was Klauss, the Alpha. He nodded at Amanda and then looked at Gene. He said in English, "I have mixed feelings about this visit, as I'm sure you understand. While I cannot forget the wrong which was done, both to my pack and to your father's pack, I have agreed to not be judgmental. I will say that knowing you two are now accepted in the New England pack does help somewhat."

He looked at John and said, "I understand your sister is now leading this New England pack. She is a Shifter but you are not?"

John answered, "Yes, that is correct. Both that she is their leader and that I am not a Shifter. My destiny lies in a different direction." He reached over to grab Tracy's hand and said, "This is where I am bound, body and soul. My life will be devoted to her."

Tracy was deeply touched by John's declaration. Wow. Just when she thought she couldn't love him any more than she already did, he overwhelmed her and made her heart explode. She rushed to say, "My soulmate likes to exaggerate. I do love him for saying that, of course. But it is his sister Missy who is gifted by the Fates for greatness."

Klauss looked at Tracy and smiled. "My information is that you are a very powerful witch. Those Fates you speak of have gifted you with supernatural abilities as well, then." Looking at everyone, he said, "All right. I do find it interesting that our Amanda has somehow ended up a member in such a distinguished pack, the largest and strongest in the U.S. I also find it interesting that this visit is somehow connected with that of Candace Axtell's visit." He looked over to Hans who had been quietly standing there during all of this. "I'm told she is here in Munich today, making speeches about justice for Johan and Justine."

Gene said, "Amanda and I now work for an anti-terrorist task force. We agreed to introduce Candace at the U.S. Embassy in Berlin since, in our former jobs, we were in America's foreign service and got to know many staff members now at that embassy. While we cannot discuss any details, it's hoped those speeches Candace is giving will lead to identifying the terrorists responsible for that bombing."

"So, your visit is part of an investigation by that task force of yours?" asked Hans. Everyone knew Candace Axtell was the niece of General Blake, who was in charge of the U.S. forces in the Mid-East. For there to

44

be some linkage between her visit and an American task force investigation was something he could see being very credible.

Amanda said, "Yes, but that's all we can probably tell you." She looked at Tracy and then back at Klauss and Hans. "Although … maybe we can trust you with just a little more information. My pack leader Missy? She and Tracy were the ones who rescued Candace last September over in Afghanistan. This task force Gene and I are working for has many resources, has been very successful against WIJO terrorists and, yeah. We will be doing everything possible to obtain justice for all those who were killed or injured at that nightclub."

This news greatly impressed both Klauss and Hans. Nothing had been more frustrating than their being completely helpless concerning the loss of their pack members and family. To realize that one of their own might possibly be taking some action was quite an eye opener and put a whole new light on things. Klauss looked at Gene and Amanda with some respect now. Then he looked at Tracy and asked, with a huge grin on his face, "Just how powerful a witch *are* you, young lady?"

John said, "Oh, she's more powerful than a locomotive! And, my sister's faster than a speeding bullet. They're Supergirls!" This got some laughs from everyone.

"I did warn you how he likes to exaggerate," said Tracy. "Even so, our task force has indeed been very successful and, as Amanda stated, we will be doing everything possible to defeat those WIJO terrorists."

They discussed the nightclub bombing but no one had any useful information. Johan and Justine had simply been in the wrong place at the wrong time and been unfortunate victims. Klauss and Hans gave assurances that if anything further was learned, it would be passed along to Amanda.

The rest of the visit went very well after that, with Amanda getting to see and be seen by everyone. There of course was plenty of food and by the time they needed to leave in order to catch the last train back to Berlin, it was agreed the day had been a very fulfilling and satisfying success.

When they boarded the train and met up with Candace and her team, their sentiment was similar. Candace and her entourage had visited all the injured victims at the various hospitals and homes for those who'd been released. The newspapers and film crews had obtained more than enough to assure coverage of the event would be in the news for several days.

Talib Mansoor had learned from his embassy source that Candace and Oliver would be back there the next day for the official tour but had gone down to Munich that day to visit the nightclub where the bombing had occurred. He had a man located in Munich and had directed him to observe the area from a distance and report what, if anything, he might see going on.

Late in the afternoon, that report came in. The Axtell girl's visit had been a big event and had received tons of media coverage. It would no doubt be the lead story that evening and have several follow-up stories for days after that. Several international outlets would surely be picking up the story and the internet coverage would be going viral.

Not only had the girl given speeches in front of the nightclub but she then had visited all the surviving victims. Plus, there was now a movement called "Justice for Jonah and Justine" which she and her group had somehow started, using the names of two of the deceased victims.

Talib considered all this to be significant enough for immediate relay to his leaders in Afghanistan. Phone calls were made and emails were sent.

Talib then waited to hear back. His team was standing by. However, no actions would be taken without getting word from higher authority.

When John and Tracy climbed into bed that night it was very, very late and they were thoroughly exhausted. As much as Tracy wanted to express her appreciation to John for the devotion he had pledged that day, she knew their libidos were not able to handle any vigorous lovemaking and she contented herself with merely climbing into John's warm embrace and snuggling up close. She decided there would definitely be some sexy times the following morning but, for right now? Falling asleep with his arms around her was all she needed and she quickly drifted off to sleep, feeling all was right in the world.

Oliver and Candace also fell asleep right away, almost before their heads hit their pillows. They too had experienced a very satisfying day.

Amanda was keyed up with excitement but, once she and Gene went to bed, they too went right to sleep with her blissful happiness quickly ebbing into peaceful slumber not long after Gene had kissed her goodnight. It had been wonderful seeing her family once again.

For Jesse and Linda, however, things were a little different. They went up to their room together and quickly got ready for bed, with Jesse undressing down to his underwear and climbing under the covers while Linda changed into her nightgown in the bathroom. She left the bathroom light on when she came out, as he had done the night before, and made her way over to her bed. The lights in the room were already turned out.

As she placed the clothing she had removed on top of the suitcase next to her bed and then climbed under the covers, she whispered, "Good night, Jesse." They had talked on and off for hours that day and she somehow felt she needed to say something.

"Good night, Linda," replied Jesse in a normal voice. He too wanted to say more and was very much aware of her being right there, in the room with him. In her bed. In her nightgown. After a long pause, he said in a much softer voice, "Sweet dreams!"

There was a short pause. Then she too whispered, "Sweet dreams, Jesse!"

Chapter Six
Wednesday, Mar 18, 2020

When Tracy joined the others for breakfast, she was feeling great. She had promised herself some sexy times when she woke up and John had not disappointed; far from it. She was aglow and ready for whatever the day might bring. She had dressed in one of her best outfits, appropriate for touring Berlin, and knew she looked good. She greeted everyone warmly as she approached their tables and, since John was following along behind, she added just a little extra sway to her hips which she knew he would appreciate.

Apparently, they were the last to arrive; even Lieutenant Saunders was there with a couple of his men, although they weren't eating but merely sitting at another table nearby. Amanda said, "I love that dress, Tracy! Come sit next to me and tell me where you bought it." She gestured to the empty seat next to her. She was alone at a table for four and had just sat down with her breakfast.

John said, "Go ahead … I'll bring you some food. I know what you want." He headed over towards the buffet dishes.

"Bring me some juice and coffee first," Tracy called out to him. Then she sat down and told Amanda, "John and I were at Quincy Market last Saturday. I found this dress at a little boutique there but I'm not sure what the store's name is. But you can't go wrong if you just check all the shops in that area. I saw lots of great buys."

"Oh, I've heard that," acknowledged Amanda. "Gene and I haven't been there yet but it's high on our list of places to see."

Tracy glanced around and was amused to see how interested Linda seemed in whatever Captain Bonomo was telling her. They were seated with Candy and Oliver at another table for four nearby. Candy was looking glamourous, as usual, with Oliver proudly at her side.

Gene was just returning with his breakfast and sat down opposite Amanda. Tracy leaned in closer and said in a conspiratorial whisper, "I don't have any enhanced senses like you guys do but, even so, I'm definitely guessing the good captain's plan for keeping things platonic with Linda might not last the week." She wiggled her eyebrows up and down and was clearly inviting them to gossip.

Gene chuckled and said, "You are incorrigible, Tracy! Amanda and I don't betray secrets. Whatever we might notice about them, or you and John for that matter, will not be shared."

"Darn! Not even a raging pheromone alert, huh?" giggled Tracy, with no embarrassment whatsoever that he and Amanda could certainly scent what she and John had been doing that morning. "That's okay. John and I have a little bet going. *Ve haf our vays of finding out!*"

John placed a glass of orange juice and a cup of coffee in front of Tracy and did the same for himself opposite to her. Hearing her last sentence where she was faking a Russian accent, he asked in a similar manner, *"Darlink! Vat mischiev are you up to now*?" Then he left to get their breakfast dishes. He returned a few minutes later with heaping plates for Tracy and himself and then took his seat.

"Thank you, thank you, thank you!" said Tracy, obviously pleased with everything he'd brought. Looking up she said, "I'm really hungry this morning and we need a good meal to start off with." She and John were taking a half-day walking tour of Berlin while the others would all be touring the embassy again.

They'd be meeting their group and an English-speaking guide at the Neue Prominade 3 which was in the center of the city's Mitte district. Lieutenant Saunders had arranged transportation for the thirty-minute ride to get there. According to Amanda, there were many historic highlights and landmarks on this tour which ought to provide them an excellent understanding of German history in relation to significant monuments, sites and buildings.

Amanda said, "As I told you yesterday, you're going to really appreciate seeing Checkpoint Charlie, the Berlin Wall, the Holocaust Memorial and all the other things on that tour. But I'm betting you'll love seeing the Brandenburg Gate the best. Then, once you've seen all those places, if you have more time? There are these hop-on, hop-off red buses where you can create your own sightseeing itinerary. These buses all have audio commentary available in English, of course."

"Yes, that's what we originally were planning on doing," said John. "But you convinced us we should start with this Discover Berlin walking tour first. Having an actual person as a guide will definitely be great."

Tracy said, "Depending on how things go after today, if we have any time here in Berlin for more sightseeing, we definitely will use those buses." They were all hoping, of course, that the terrorist group would reveal something about itself and they'd be busy following up on leads rather than merely sightseeing.

Talib Mansoor was getting more and more complaints from the members in his group. Most had only come to Germany recently after extensive training in Afghanistan. He and three others had established both their terrorist cell and liquor store business in Leipzig two years earlier, getting financial assistance from WIJO for that purpose.

Leipzig had a population of six hundred thousand and was a good central location about a hundred miles southwest of Berlin, two hundred fifty miles northeast of Frankfurt and two hundred seventy miles north of Munich. In addition to his store, he now had a large warehouse and several vehicles for making deliveries throughout Germany. He had worked hard to build up his distribution since it made an excellent cover for the attacks which he intended to carry out. The recent members of his cell were easily absorbed into the business as warehouse workers and deliverymen. Keeping all their various munitions hidden away had been easy. The nightclub bombing in Munich had been executed exactly as planned. Mansoor was certain his ambitions for advancing in WIJO would all be coming true.

Thus, he was not willing to allow any complaints to influence him. He was a patient man and had worked too long and too hard to arrange things the way they were in Germany. He had earned the confidence of Mullah Ahmed Kahtar and the other leaders and was not about to take any actions which might risk all he had accomplished. It was enough that Kahtar was willing to wait and see. Hopefully, this visit by Candace Axtell and her demon fiancé would not amount to anything and all the media hype would quickly die down. Then the additional bombings already planned could resume.

He called Kahtar on their secure satellite phone link to brief him on the latest news concerning this visit. Although, satellite phones do disclose exact GPS locations in an insecure manner and can be traced, it was considered secure enough since the calls were encrypted, with no risk of being intercepted and listened to by any high-tech equipment.

After exchanging greetings, Kahtar asked, "What news do you have today about the American visitors, my friend?"

"As expected, they have spent all day at the U.S. Embassy," Mansoor told him. "The girl gave more speeches there denouncing WIJO and hoping this movement she started yesterday in Munich will continue, even after she leaves. Justice for Johan and Justine. These American infidels love to stir things up with their slogans."

"Do you know what they plan next?"

"Unfortunately, no. They did not say anything about that and all I know is their military guards will still be with them for several days, wherever they go."

Kahtar grunted. "Her uncle will not allow them to travel anywhere otherwise. And, of course, that demon Bessom has proven what he can do. But, the girl attends college and this trip sounds like only something she's doing while her school is on vacation this week."

"It is good you are keeping track of her like that," said Mansoor. "Once she is gone, we are ready here to continue our bombings. The new members of my group are complaining, however. They are very anxious to take action and are not happy they must wait."

"Talib, remind them we are anxious as well but have been interfered with many times now by these demons the U.S. is using against us. Oliver Bessom is a huge threat and so is Missy McCrea. Since West Point cadets are also on vacation this week, it's very possible McCrea is right there with them along with who knows what other demons. Tell everyone in your group to do as they're told. For now? We shall continue to wait and see."

Tracy slid into the booth and John followed along next to her. They had picked a restaurant their guide Frank had recommended which was famous for its wiener schnitzel and beer. They each ordered a dark beer right away while they reviewed the menu; the drinking age everywhere in Germany was only eighteen so they had no problem ordering after showing their id's.

"Frank considered it mandatory we experience some of the wonderful beer this country is so famous for," said Tracy. "He really was great. I'm so glad we listened to Amanda and went on this walking tour."

"Yeah, only my feet are ready to fall off," said John. "I freely admit I can't sustain the pace the way you highly trained West Point cadets can. But, yeah … that tour was fascinating and Frank was perfect. He really knew his German history and had an answer for every question anyone asked today."

"What are you going to eat? I'm getting the wiener schnitzel, just like he suggested. The way he described it being so tender and perfectly breaded … not too cakey or too thin?"

John nodded and said, "Me too. If it's as crisp and bursting with flavor as he says, then we're in for a real treat. My stomach started growling after he told us all that."

"Of course, since we skipped lunch, your stomach would probably growl at just about anything." Tracy put down her menu and watched as the waiter served their drinks. After they placed their orders and the waiter left, she took a long drink from her beer. "Ahhh, that's good. Really, really good!"

John tasted his beer and was equally as impressed. Then he said, "Taking this trip with you just gets better and better. Many magic moments and magnificent memories!"

"Yes, so far. I almost feel guilty having so much fun while everyone else is working hard to find those terrorists."

"Well, hopefully they'll succeed and maybe then you'll be asked to help." John was proud of the way she wanted to do her part. "It's not up to you to do it all, you know. It's enough that what you can do will make a difference and that you're willing to do that."

"I suppose. Did you notice how proud Amanda's parents were when Klauss learned she was working for a task force?" asked Tracy. "When their Alpha realized their daughter was helping, was actually doing something about what happened to Johan and Justine ..."

"Exactly. And, all the publicity which Candy is getting, demanding justice for them, will surely lead to something."

Just then their waiter was back with their order and they watched as he set their dishes in front of them. As they enjoyed their meal they again were thankful they'd had Frank as their guide that day. It was every bit as delicious as he'd described.

Chapter Seven
Mar 18, 2020

Captain Bonomo and Linda had just gone up to their room when Lieutenant Colonel Schermerhorn's call came in. They sat down side by side on Linda's bed and Jesse said, "Go ahead, Colonel. We have you on speakerphone."

"Good news. Missy was able to listen to a call from someone named Talib which was about Candy and Oliver's visit today at the embassy. He mentioned his group being ready to continue the bombings once you all leave Germany. They're concerned about interference from demons and are waiting until then before taking any actions."

"That is good news that Missy managed hearing that," said Linda, looking at Jesse and grinning. They knew Missy would not only have been invisible, spying on various WIJO leaders in Afghanistan, but was also fluent in Pashto and thus able to listen to everything with her supernatural hearing. "Obviously, our being here triggered that call. Have you traced it back to a location?"

"Yes. We already know it was from somewhere in Leipzig and by morning we should have an exact address. If Talib is associated with that address, we can also identify him by his full name."

Jesse said, "Great, sir. Leipzig is less than three hours from here. I'll let our security team know we'll need them to escort us there tomorrow morning. They have several guards here already but Lieutenant Saunders told me he has more on standby at Ansbach and that he'd want them to travel with us in the event we went anywhere like this."

They discussed the plan with the lieutenant colonel for a few minutes and then he disconnected so they could make arrangements with the others. Linda said she'd call the other three couples while Jesse called Lieutenant Saunders. They were both pretty excited and, in the euphoria of the moment, Linda gave Jesse a quick hug. Then she went into their bathroom to make her calls.

After speaking to Candace, Amanda and Tracy, she was feeling even more excited and keyed up. She went back into their room and saw that Jesse had finished his call, had gotten undressed and into bed, but was still wide awake and sitting up. There was still one light on over by the small desk but it wasn't very bright. She smiled at him and said, "Let me get some of my things and then I'll get ready for bed. Be back in a minute."

Linda brought her suitcase into the bathroom and got undressed. Then, deciding the time was right for this, rather than putting on the modest nightgown she'd worn the first two nights, she instead put on the sheer, sexy, babydoll lingerie she'd brought along, just in case.

It had been more than two years since she'd been in any relationship and she was definitely feeling aroused and drawn to Jesse. They had shared a lot of personal information and she knew he hadn't been with anyone for a long time either. She'd explained how her last boyfriend had been a werewolf and why she'd broken up with him. She'd never thought she'd be able to share those details with anyone but, with Jesse? Somehow, it had been easy telling him everything.

She was fairly sure she'd read all the signals he'd been giving. He was attracted to her but would never force anything and was waiting. So, she hoped *she* could force things, rather than wait any longer. With some nervous anticipation now mixed in with all the excitement she was already feeling, she left the bathroom and went back into their dimly lit room.

When Jesse saw Linda come out wearing a different nightgown he noticed right away. It was impossible not to notice the see through nightie she was now wearing and he immediately got aroused. She pretended nothing was different and carried her suitcase back to where she'd had it before without glancing in his direction. He knew she was definitely checking for his reaction, however.

"You know, a guy can't ignore how a beautiful, curvy woman looks, no matter how platonic he's promised he'd keep things, when she sashays into his room wearing what you're wearing right now, Linda."

"Oh? I'm sorry! Am I making things difficult for you, Jesse?" asked Linda in a soft, sexy voice which was definitely feigning innocence. "Of course ... maybe the

60

woman isn't interested in keeping things platonic." Her voice now was definitely *not* innocent. "Maybe she doesn't want to be ignored."

"Is that so? Well, why don't you sashay right over here, then." Jesse shifted position so there was room next to him on the bed, pulled back the covers and patted the mattress. He'd been hoping all the feelings he'd been harboring for days now might be mutual. She was making it very obvious that indeed they were.

"Are you sure, Jesse? I mean … we don't have to do this," said Linda with some hesitation. "We …"

Jesse didn't wait but got up and went over to where she was standing. "If you want this anywhere near as much as I want this, then we definitely *do* have to do this." He pulled her close and looked into her eyes with a big smile on his face.

She welcomed him without any further hesitation and pulled his head down with both hands so she could kiss him. Their kiss quickly deepened into something very powerful as their desperately needy passions were ignited and they began pressing their bodies against one another harder and harder. The babydoll nightie did not stay on Linda for very long and they quickly tumbled back into Jesse's bed.

Tracy got off the phone with Linda and smiled at John. "You heard that, right?" They were returning in the vehicle Lieutenant Saunders had sent for them and were almost back. It was late and they'd had a fabulous time. From the excitement in her voice, the news had clearly just made things even better.

"Yes, I heard you say we're leaving in the morning for Leipzig," replied John. "Obviously, the task force received some good Intel. Did my sister have anything to do with that?"

Tracy glanced at the two soldiers in the front seat and said, "Yeah, she did. I'll explain about that later. What matters is we now have people and places to check out. We should know more when we meet for breakfast. There will be some additional security guys here then to go with us."

"As much as I love sightseeing, I know this is why we're really here. Progress is good." John wrapped an arm around her and pulled her close. With her head resting on his shoulder he whispered in her ear, "We need to celebrate this, right?"

Tracy giggled and whispered, "Can't wait!" They remained quiet while cuddling during the short time it took to reach the Clay Compound and then thanked the two men for bringing them back and went up to their room.

They quickly got ready for bed. When Tracy came out of the bathroom, she was naked and said, "Let the celebration begin!" Then she flounced over to the bed and climbed under the covers where John was waiting for her, also naked. She crawled on top of him and began kissing his lips with fervor, her tongue teasing and probing.

John kissed her back for a couple minutes and then pushed her higher so he could reach one of her nipples with his mouth, teasing and sucking on that with his lips and tongue while tweaking her other nipple with his fingers. He paused briefly to mumble, "I *love* celebration sex with you, Tracy. Always such fun!" Then he began nibbling on each of her pebbled nipples, alternating back and forth while running his hands down to massage and squeeze her rear.

Tracy moaned appreciatively as her body quickly responded to everything he was doing and she felt herself getting wet, throbbing and aching for more. She rolled onto her back and spread her legs, signaling him the foreplay was over and she wanted him inside of her.

But John was in no hurry and slipped one arm underneath her while he continued working on one of her breasts with his mouth, sliding his other hand down to caress her mound. He used his fingers to slowly bring her to an exquisite orgasm before he finally rolled on top and pushed himself inside.

Tracy was always loud and noisy during their lovemaking and the more she and John had sex, the more uninhibited she had become. She wrapped her legs around him and begged him, "Give it to me!", "Harder, harder!", "Ohh, ohhhhh, *there*!" and "Faster, *faster*!"

She met each of his thrusts with her pelvis rocking back and forth, demanding more and more. She was thankful he'd known one orgasm would not be enough for her on this particular night. And, as he began increasing the pace, she felt her next orgasm starting to build, making her quake in anticipation. She began bucking her hips underneath him with even greater motion, yelling and hollering while John grunted his pleasure up above. When her orgasm finally hit, its explosive power was overwhelming and she yowled her pleasure while sensing his release right afterwards.

This time, she was done and as they both regained their breath, she made small mewling noises. When her spasms subsided, they were followed by some delicious little aftershocks and she cried out softly with each one. They both gradually began drifting off to sleep, still entwined in one another's arms with Tracy's face nestled against John's chest and their bodies pressed tightly together.

While barely conscious, Tracy rolled over and pressed herself back against John, now spooned around her. He hugged her close and cupped one of her breasts. Then they both slept deeply and peacefully until the next morning.

Chapter Eight
Thursday, Mar 19, 2020

There was an air of excitement at breakfast as they all greeted one another, made their selections and sat down to eat. The first phase of their trip had been successful and it was now time for the next phase. After quickly eating, they gathered together with Lieutenant Saunders and his security team in an empty conference room where they could talk freely. Everyone found a place to sit and waited.

Lieutenant Saunders started by introducing each of them and explaining that Linda Rayburn would brief them on their mission and answer any questions. He assured Linda that all of his men had been cleared for this special assignment and sworn to secrecy. Then he sat down as Linda came forward and faced everyone.

She began by saying, "First, I want to thank Lieutenant Saunders and his security team for being here and supporting us. Our little team here are members of a special task force which deals with WIJO terrorists. That task force has interfered with several WIJO attacks, stopping them with very limited publicity so the outside world was largely unaware of the extent of, or the full threat from, those particular attacks. Unfortunately, the attack here in Munich took place without our being able to do that.

"Our task force is secret and now has representatives from several U.S. government agencies as well as from the U.S. military. It began when Candace Axtel was kidnapped last year," Linda paused to nod briefly at Candace and then continued, "which I'm sure everyone here remembers. It has stopped attacks and dealt with WIJO terrorists in Afghanistan, the U.S., the U.K. and … with your help … will do so here in Germany. Any questions so far?" She paused to look around at her audience.

One soldier raised his hand and then asked, "So, are you *all* members of this secret task force?" He looked over doubtfully at Tracy and it was obvious he was surprised to see people so young being included.

"Well, I'm glad you asked that. I want to elaborate just a bit on what roles each of us have over here. Candace, as you have seen, has been speaking out and trying to provoke the terrorists. That has been successful, which I'll get to in a minute. Her fiancé Oliver has been a task force member going back to when she was missing. He and Tracy helped locate and rescue her, but those details and most of what they do on our task force are highly classified. Tracy also speaks Pashto, which she has been studying as a cadet at West Point."

There were some appreciative murmurings as many heads turned to look over at Tracy. There was a growing atmosphere of respect towards Linda and her team.

Linda said, "Captain Bonomo is a TAC Officer at West Point. He and John have provided support on some missions for which the details are also highly classified. Gene and Amanda Tremblay are members of our task force as well. They speak several languages.

Amanda is originally from Germany and she and her family knew Jonah and Justine personally." The media had been widely broadcasting Candy's call for justice, with Jonah and Justine now martyrs for the cause.

Another soldier raised his hand. "You mentioned Ms. Axtel has been successful in provoking the terrorists here in Germany. But, none of us have seen anything as yet."

"That's right," said Linda. "Since WIJO has been embarrassed on several occasions now when going after Candace, their leaders have given strict orders to the group here in Germany to stay away from her and wait until she leaves. Then they will continue with further bombing attacks. One of our task force members in Afghanistan was able to overhear those orders being given during a phone conversation yesterday. Our support team back in the U.S. has been able to trace that phone call back to an address in Leipzig, which is where we'll all be going right after this briefing."

This news got everyone excited and there were several cheers.

"The call to Afghanistan was from an apartment building which has several residents. However, only one of them is named Talib which is what the WIJO leader called the person he gave those orders to. Talib Mansoor lives in apartment four-eighteen on the top floor. Further checking shows he's been running a liquor store with an extensive distribution network for the past couple of years. But that business is actually owned by a holding company. Our task force worked all night getting this info and will continue researching this holding company. However, it fits the pattern for other WIJO cells." Linda paused to let everyone process what she'd told them.

One of the soldiers asked, "Can't the German authorities act on this? I mean ... surely they want to find these terrorists, right?"

Linda answered, "There's not enough evidence for them as yet. Our task force is keeping them in the loop. But, all we really have so far is a phone conversation which was overheard but not recorded. That's why my team is going to these addresses in Leipzig. We hope we can find more evidence which the authorities can then use." She looked over to Lieutenant Saunders and said, "That's as much as we can share with you and your men at this point. Our team here will want your support, of course, but we need to have the lead on all of this."

"Absolutely, ma'am! No problem," said the lieutenant. He stood up and signaled for his men to leave the room.

"Good. There are some classified things I wish to discuss with my team. Then, we'll check out of here and join you in your vehicles." Linda knew from what Jesse had told her, based on his conversations earlier with the lieutenant, that they would be travelling in eight different vehicles. Most of the soldiers were wearing civilian clothes with concealed weapons. She watched as the men filed out. Once the last man closed the door, she turned back to her team.

Oliver asked, "What's the plan for our getting more evidence, Linda?"

"Well, as I mentioned, the task force is still researching that holding company. They're also checking out that liquor business. They have a few employee names but it seems there are quite a few part time workers without documentation. Again, Robert's team has only had a few hours so far."

"Meanwhile, we can get up close and personal and maybe use our supernatural abilities to determine a few things, right?" asked Tracy.

Linda smiled and said, "Exactly." She looked at Oliver, Gene and Amanda and added, "Once Oliver gets close enough to experience Talib's essence and our werewolves have his scent … we can hopefully identify who else are members of his group, where they live, where they work, and eventually perhaps locate whatever weapons and munitions Talib's group must have stored away."

Candace said, "I'll be more than happy to confront them face-to-face if that will help."

"That's good of you to offer, Candy, but let's try doing a few other things first," said Linda. "Can Oliver wear any disguise? Perhaps take his glasses off and wear a hat? I'd like to have him get close to Talib but keep you out of it, for now."

They all chatted about various approaches they could use for a few minutes but then agreed they needed to get going. They checked out of their rooms, brought their bags out to the vehicles waiting for them and then, pairing off into four of the vehicles, they were soon on their way to Leipzig.

Talib Mansoor had been nervous and uneasy after the phone call with Mullah Ahmed Kahtar the day before. Kahtar had warned it was possible other demons might be with the Axtell girl, in addition to Oliver Bessom. Meanwhile, he'd received more complaints from those in his group who were restless and wanted to resume their bombings.

Ravi understood why Talib was upset. They'd been talking about the situation and he assured him the dissidents in their group would behave themselves. He tried to explain things, saying, "Look, the nightclub in Munich was a big success for them and they're unhappy the media is now focusing on what this Candace Axtell is saying rather than the message they wanted."

Only Ravi, Tabish and Musa, the three men who'd been with Talib the past two years, were allowed to come to work in his store that day. They each had valid documents and had established residence, like he had. The others did not and posed a definite risk. Tabash was at the cash register while Musa was bringing more cases of beer in from the rear.

"Their happiness does not matter," countered Talib as he watched Ravi arrange some wine bottles on the shelf. He had instructed all of the new group members to stay out of sight either at his warehouse or at their apartments and continue waiting. "Our leaders

70

are very concerned that what happened to other groups will happen to our group. These demons might be anywhere and cannot be stopped."

Just as Talib had his sources, some of the new members in their group had their own sources. They had all learned Candace Axtell and Oliver Bessom had checked out that morning and departed from the compound where they'd been staying. They had left in several vehicles believed to be operated by the U.S. Army. However, their destination was unknown. They may have left Berlin. They may have left Germany. This news had added a great deal of tension. They might be anywhere.

Ravi was in the middle of this discussion with Talib while four strangers were looking around in the store. They had come in a few minutes earlier. One couple was in their thirties and obviously married, with the wife complaining to the man about something in German. They had entered with the other couple who were much younger; the girl looked to be in her late teens. Based on their appearance, however, it was obvious these strangers would not understand anything being said since the conversation was all in Pashto. He told Talib, "We should continue this later. You have customers." Then, in German, he said to the young girl who was nearby, "Can I help you with anything?"

She smiled and shook her head while the other woman answered in German from the next aisle, "My cousin and her boyfriend aren't buying anything; they're merely with me and my husband." She headed towards the register with her husband carrying two wine bottles behind her.

Talib glanced at them dismissively and looked back at Ravi. "Tabash can handle any purchases," he muttered in Pashto. Then he added, "Finish up here and go check on our men. Make sure they stay at home and out of sight. You keep saying they will not go against my orders but I'm not so sure. Especially that Dhanial. He's been acting like he's their leader and I don't trust him."

Amanda paid for the wine and then she, Gene, Tracy and Oliver made their way outside. Once they had all gotten into the sedan and were driving away, she looked at Tracy and said, "You looked as though you'd heard enough. Was that Pashto they were speaking?"

"Oh, yes! And they were talking about us, believe it or not. The one in charge, who must be Talib, was saying we demons might be anywhere and cannot be stopped." Tracy giggled and looked at Oliver, who had put his glasses back on. She asked, "Were you able to sense enough energy from each of them?"

Oliver nodded and said, "Yeah, I can find any of those four men now."

"Amanda and I will recognize their scent as well," said Gene. "Working together, I'm sure we can locate where each one is staying."

Tracy said, "Talib asked that one guy to leave and go check on the others. We need to follow him. Hopefully, we'll learn where all of them are staying."

Chapter Nine
Mar 19, 2020

After dropping Amanda and Tracy off at the hotel in downtown Leipzig which Lieutenant Saunders had selected for everyone, Gene and Oliver drove back to begin surveillance of the liquor store. They intended to follow the man Tracy had told them would be checking on others.

As the girls headed up to Linda and Jesse's room to join them along with Candy and John, Tracy smirked and said, "I won the bet, didn't I?"

Amanda sighed, knowing which bet Tracy was referring to. "Gene and I explained we do not disclose private things like that about people."

"What's to disclose? They made it clear enough when we checked in here, right? They wanted the same room and there was no mention of being platonic this time."

Amanda rolled her eyes but had nothing to say. On arriving at the room, they knocked and were welcomed inside.

Candy asked, "Do you think anyone recognized Oliver?"

"No, he was totally ignored," said Amanda. "I think the guys were too busy checking out Tracy. They

73

spoke freely in front of us. They definitely are members of the WIJO group which bombed that nightclub."

Jesse said, "I'll let Lieutenant Saunders know. He has some men watching the liquor store and others watching Talib's apartment building. He'll want to keep that up."

"Yes, and he has GPS tracking in the car Gene and Oliver are using, right?" asked Amanda. "They hope one of the men will be leading them back to where other members are hiding out."

"Great," said Jesse, nodding in affirmation. Looking at Linda he said, "Tell them what Dale Hewson has learned for us."

"The holding company which owns the liquor store has ties with another company which owns a large warehouse about forty minutes outside of the city here," said Linda. "Dale says that's probably where the business gets most of its revenue, with the store merely a front. In order to be distributing the quantity of beer and wine which this company seems to be delivering throughout its network, a large place is needed for inventory and for storing all their vehicles."

"Hey, that's great," said Tracy. "Amanda will recognize if the guys we met today have been there. Once we confirm that, we need to search for whatever might be stored there besides booze."

They discussed various options for getting inside and doing a search but, until they actually got to see what they were dealing with, they really couldn't agree on any specific plan. However, Tracy said she and Amanda would try something similar to what they'd done in the liquor store. They decided Linda and Candy would stay behind and maintain communications with everyone while Jesse, Amanda, Tracy and John went out to take a look at the warehouse.

Lieutenant Saunders sat up front in the passenger seat of the lead vehicle which also had John and Jesse in it. For this recon, they were using four vehicles after leaving several men behind to guard Candace; one of the vehicles was a car they'd just rented for Tracy and Amanda. He asked, "When we get to this warehouse, what's the plan?"

Jesse said, "Once we do a drive-by, Amanda and Tracy will circle back and fake having car problems. The rental car they selected has a simple distributor cap held down with two clips. Tracy says she can pop that cap off using the nail file in her purse, remove the rotor and reinstall the cap in less than a minute. Then, should anyone try to help them, the car won't start."

"So that's why you wanted her to pick out the rental car. I thought the rental was only so the registration wouldn't trace back to one of our military vehicles."

"Well, that too, but they wanted to be sure they could easily disable it. It's not likely anyone will attempt to do any actual troubleshooting but they might need to show they can't get it started. Once they've faked breaking down, they'll approach the place on foot.

Amanda can speak German and will tell them their car stalled out and now won't start."

The lieutenant nodded and said, "Okay. That gets them inside the place. And, since Tracy knows Pashto, she'll be able to listen to any meaningful conversations, just like she did at that liquor store."

John said, "They figure they can ask whoever is there to call a tow truck for them. Hopefully, while they're waiting for that to show up, there might be some conversations worth listening to. If they can manage to do any snooping around as well, that'll be a plus."

"If they have any trouble with whoever is there," said Jesse, "they'll send us a text message and you can have your guys rush in to rescue them. But we don't really expect that to happen. They're just a couple of girls who need a tow, right?" He grinned.

After Tracy had the distributor cap back on with its two clips reattached, she had Amanda grind away on the starter a few times. So far, so good. They left the car with the hood still up and headed over to the warehouse they'd found at the address Linda had provided.

They'd selected a spot for their breakdown that was a hundred yards from the main entrance. There was a large paved area containing several cars, trucks and vans parked all along one side. There were also four loading bays on that side but none had their doors open.

None had been open when they'd gone by earlier either. However, there were lights shining through the windows near the office door at the end of the building. That, the parked cars and an open main gate, suggested there probably were some people in there.

They'd all stopped at a convenient location about two miles past the warehouse and discussed what they'd noticed. The place had a large fence all around it and they'd noticed two surveillance cameras; most likely there were others. Getting in undetected didn't look good.

Tracy's plan seemed feasible and, not seeing any other way to get into the place, it was decided to proceed with it. While the location was remote and the men inside the warehouse were members of a terrorist group, they would have no reason to suspect Amanda and Tracy of anything. Thus, the risk seemed minimal.

On the way back, as they'd approached the spot they'd selected to stop their car, Tracy had asked, "Amanda, are you sure you're okay with our doing this? We can keep going and just tell the guys we changed our mind. Even though everyone agrees we should be okay in there ..."

Amanda had laughed and said, "Look, I'm fine with everything and really want to do just as we planned. I mean ... it's like what I told Gene. I'm with the girl who can *incinerate* anyone who might want to hurt me, right? What can go wrong?"

Tracy had said, "Geez! And here I was thinking I was okay since you'd be ripping their throats out as a wolf. All righty then! Let's do this!"

Now, after walking up to the office door, they were committed. It was late in the afternoon and time to become damsels in distress. The door was not locked and as they went inside, Amanda called out in German, "Hello? Is anyone here? We need some help ... our car broke down."

There was a long counter which was mostly empty except for a computer monitor and keyboard. There were no chairs in front but on the other side, in a back corner, there was a single desk. The desk had several piles of paper, another computer monitor and keyboard as well as a telephone sitting on it. There was an empty chair behind the desk with two more empty chairs in front. Cases and cases of beer were stacked all around in several places. Then, there was a doorway which led back into the rest of the warehouse.

There had not been any bell over the entry but, on the counter, there was a button with a prominent sign which stated in German, "Ring for service". They pressed that and waited.

After less than a minute, two men came through the back doorway and approached. They were somewhere in their twenties although one looked somewhat older than the other. They had beards, were dressed in work clothes and did not appear very friendly. The older one demanded, in heavily accented

German, "What do you want?" It was obvious the girls were not welcome.

Amanda said, "Our car broke down and we need to call a tow truck but we don't know where we are or who to call. Can you help us?"

"Where is your car and what is wrong with it?"

Amanda walked towards the window next to the outside door and pointed. "See? We are right there. It stalled and now it won't start."

The younger man asked, "Do you need gasoline? Maybe you ran out." His German was also heavily accented.

"No, no. We have more than half a tank. I don't know what is wrong. Can you help us call for a tow?"

The men were not pleased and looked at each other. The older man grumbled in Pashto, "We don't need this right now. See if you can get them going." Then, looking at Amanda, he said in German, "Tariq will look at it for you." He gestured to the younger man to go out and look. Amanda went outside with him while Tracy remained inside, pacing aimlessly in the limited space in front of the counter. The man didn't seem interested in talking to her, which was good. However, he did keep a close watch on her which, since he seemed to be undressing her with his eyes, wasn't so good.

Five minutes later, Tariq returned with Amanda right behind him. He announced, in Pashto, "It will not start. You should probably call Talib. He will know what to do." He went back around to the other side of the counter where the older man was waiting. "I wrote down the license number in case Talib wants that." He handed over a piece of paper.

The older man grunted as he took the paper. Then he said, also in Pashto, "I don't like this. We will be stuck here until Talib arranges for a tow truck to come out. What are we supposed to do with these two women?" Turning to look at Amanda, he said in German, "I must call my boss. He will know who to call." With a shrug, he added, "We are new here." Then he walked back to the desk, picked up the phone and dialed a number.

Tracy was only able to hear part of what the man was saying, but she did hear him say Talib's name and it was clear he was providing an explanation of their situation, to include reading off the license number of their car. After a couple of minutes, he finished and hung up. When he returned, he told Amanda someone would be coming in an hour or so. Maybe longer.

Amanda said, "Thank you, thank you." Turning to Tracy, she told her about the tow truck coming in French. Although neither of them was all that fluent in French, she had picked up enough living with Gene, who was fluent, and she knew Tracy could manage a few words as well. She hoped these men were not very familiar with the language and, watching their expressions as she talked to Tracy, it looked as though they weren't. Switching to German, she told the older man and Tariq, "My cousin is from Paris and doesn't know very much German."

Both men seemed to accept this. Since Tracy hadn't said anything up until now, this explanation probably made sense to them. They both studied Tracy with interest but, since she was now removing her coat and folding it over one arm, that interest seemed directed more at her trim female figure than at whether or not she could speak German.

After watching them looking at Tracy for a few moments, Amanda glanced around the room and then asked, "Can we use a restroom, please?"

This request apparently caught the older man by surprise. Where was his mind and what had he been thinking about?

Tariq chuckled and said in Pashto, "Saeed, you must let them use our facilities. I doubt they can wait until the tow truck gets here before they can relieve themselves, right?" He turned and headed toward the doorway leading back into the warehouse. "I will tell Dhanial and the others to stay out of sight until we can bring these women back out here."

Saeed grunted and said, also in Pashto, "Make sure nobody tries anything with them. Talib was very clear … we need to avoid drawing attention to ourselves until we know it's safe."

The younger man stopped and looked back, answering, "Sure, but if Dhanial gets a good look at them ... especially that young pretty one ..."

"Make sure he doesn't," snapped Saeed. "He's not supposed to even be here. If Talib ..."

"Yeah, yeah. I know. I'll make sure," interrupted Tariq as he turned and continued on into the warehouse. Not long after the door closed behind him, the sounds of muffled shouting could be heard. Then it quieted down.

Turning to Amanda and Tracy, Saeed said, "He will be right back to show you where our restroom is. He's just checking to make sure it's available for you right now." Then he went over to the desk and sat down. He began studying the monitor while moving a mouse around and clicking some keys on the keyboard.

He sent brief glances over at the two women while he quickly reviewed the various surveillance camera views during the past thirty minutes. He was annoyed with himself for not closing and locking the gate after Dhanial had shown up with three others an hour earlier. Talib was not going to be happy about that and, now that these women had shown up, his day was just that much more complicated.

He also was annoyed with himself about all the things that French girl was making him think about. He had not been with any woman since coming to Germany and seeing how attractive she was ... well ... he couldn't help getting an erection just seeing her take off that coat.

Chapter Ten

Mar 19, 2020

When Ravi knocked on the door at one of the two apartments being used by Dhanial and the others, there was no answer. This was not good. He quickly went to the other apartment and knocked on its door. When it opened, he rushed inside without waiting and, after a quick look around, immediately demanded to know where everyone was.

Only Saeed and one other man was supposed to be over at the warehouse. The other nine men in the group were supposed to be holed up in these two apartments, laying low. It was obvious Dhanial and three others were not there.

After questioning the five remaining men, he realized Talib had been right to be worried. Dhanial intended to carry out the next phase of their planned attacks. He was picking up some of the bombing devices at the warehouse and would be bringing them to their next target, a club in Frankfort, using one of Talib's vans. After learning Candace Axtell and her group had checked out of the rooms they'd been staying at and had left Berlin, Dhanial had convinced himself and the three who had gone with him there was no reason to delay any longer.

Ravi immediately called Talib and let him know.

After some heavy cursing, Talib said, "I just talked to Saeed. He didn't say anything about Dhanial being at the warehouse."

Ravi said, "Well, Dhanial can be rather intimidating. He claims he's got friends high up in the organization back in Afghanistan. What were you talking to Saeed about, anyway?"

"He had me send a tow truck out there to pick up a car and the two women who were in it when it broke down. You better get out there right away. Bring the five guys you have there with you. I want everyone together in one place. I'll call Saeed and insist he stop Dhanial from going anywhere until you get there. I'd go myself but we just got a delivery here at the store which I need to take care of before I can leave."

"Okay," agreed Ravi. "I'll try to keep everyone right at the warehouse until you can get out there later on. I'll remind them all that you are getting orders directly from Mullah Ahmed Kahtar."

Oliver and Gene had parked their car two blocks away from where Ravi had parked. Then they'd made their way back on foot to the apartment building Ravi had entered. They had no difficulty identifying the building and found they could walk inside without any problem; they were in a poor section of town and the lack of security wasn't a surprise.

Following Ravi's scent, they made their way up to the two apartments which he'd visited. Gene spent several minutes outside of each one scenting the various persons who had recently been into these units. In addition to Ravi and the three others Gene had noted at the liquor store, he scented there were eleven more men total but no women. He knew one apartment was empty at the moment with Ravi inside the other one with five of these eleven men. Since they'd been briefed by Linda while driving over, he knew about the warehouse outside the city and guessed that was where the missing six guys might be.

Just as they were leaving so they could call Linda with what they'd learned, they heard the apartment door open. They ducked out the door at the end of the corridor and waited. Sure enough, Ravi and the five others all came out and headed towards them. They quickly went up one flight of stairs to keep out of sight. After the others went down and left the building, they followed after them. They waited until Ravi's car along with one other car started up and drove away. Then they exited the building and walked back to their car.

Oliver called Linda so she could arrange for surveillance at this apartment, in addition to the unit they knew was Talib's across town. When she asked if they could follow Ravi to see if he was going out to the warehouse, he said, "No problem. I have his energy signature and can follow that to wherever he's going."

Linda explained, "If he's going out to the warehouse, I hope he doesn't arrive until after Amanda and Tracy have left. They're out there right now, waiting for a tow truck. Ravi will recognize them if he gets there before they've left. I'll text them and alert everyone else what's happening while you and Gene are following Ravi." Then she gave him the address for the warehouse.

When Amanda and Tracy were finally led out back and shown where the restroom was, they took a good look around the warehouse. It was mostly wide open with a ceiling about thirty feet up. Along one side, they could see there were four loading bays which lined up with the doors they'd noted on the outside. Three bays were empty but the one closest to them had a van parked inside. The warehouse contained many crates and stacks of boxes along with shelves filled with more boxes. They could see there were a few doors along the opposite side of the warehouse which probably were for offices or storage rooms. They assumed that was where the other guys had gone.

Once inside the restroom, Amanda said, "I can scent four men are here besides the two we've already met."

Tracy nodded and said, "Yeah, and one of them must be Dhanial. I heard Saeed mention his name when he told Tariq to have everyone hide from us."

"Wait, isn't that the name I heard Talib mention back in the liquor store?" asked Amanda. "I didn't understand what he was saying but …"

"Talib was saying Dhanial was supposed to be at home. That's who he asked Ravi to go and check on. I don't think he's supposed to be out here today. Let me text Linda with what we've noticed so far." Tracy pulled out her phone and saw she had received a couple of texts with the most recent one being from Linda. "Hey, she just sent both of us a message ... let's see what she's got to say."

Amanda pulled out her phone and they both read how Ravi was now headed out in their direction. She said, "Oh, oh! We might need to fix our car and leave before that tow truck gets here. We don't want to be recognized."

"Let's see what else we can learn about this warehouse before we do that. We have some time yet. I'll see if I can distract Tariq while you sniff around with that wolfy nose of yours." Tracy unbuttoned the top two buttons on her blouse. While she didn't have the biggest boobs in the world, she knew the curves she did have would still be of interest to Tariq from the way she'd been ogled when she'd removed her coat.

"Good idea," agreed Amanda. "I'll start with that van. Send your text and then let's go."

Tracy quickly sent Linda an update and then lead the way back out of the restroom. Sure enough, as she sidled up to Tariq and began talking nonsense in French, she totally had him mesmerized. When she began asking him questions, pointing at some of the boxes stacked nearby while invading his personal space with her closeness, he was definitely affected and paid very little attention to where Amanda was.

Amanda quickly headed over to the van and began registering everything she could scent. She distinctly noted the four individuals she'd not seen yet who had just been in the area. While she could not see inside the van, there was an odor coming from it which she had learned to associate with munitions and explosives. It was quite unique and different from all the various odors in the warehouse from beer, wine and liquor bottles and she began tracking it back away from the van.

Just as she was approaching one of the storeroom doors where the unique odor seemed strongest, the man Tracy had been distracting finally noticed where Amanda was going and began yelling at her. She quickly turned back and headed towards him and Tracy, feigning innocence. She said, "My cousin said she wanted a few moments alone with you ..." She let that thought hang there, unfinished, hoping whatever act Tracy had been putting on had been convincing enough.

Tracy grabbed the guy's arm and hugged it tight, up against one of her breasts, and said something in French which neither she nor the man understood. Tariq did notice her firm breast pressing against his arm, however, as she led him back towards the office. Amanda followed along behind with the guy again paying her very little attention. Yea, Tracy!

On re-entering the office, Saeed barked at Tariq in Pashto, "What took so long?" Then, without waiting for an answer, he continued, "Stay here with these women while I go back and talk to the others. Talib called and is very upset. He wants me to make sure they stay here."

"You better hurry then," replied Tariq. "I think Dhanial is almost ready to leave. They were just finishing up when I asked them to get out of sight."

Saeed cursed and rushed back into the warehouse without paying any attention to Amanda or Tracy. Amanda walked over to the chair behind the desk and sat down, taking advantage of how Tracy was now again keeping Tariq occupied. When she glanced at the monitor, she could see several surveillance views of both the exterior as well as a couple views showing inside the warehouse. In his haste to go talk to the men back there, Saeed had been too distracted to hide these views.

Tracy worked her way over to one of the two chairs in front of the desk, pulling Tariq along with her and getting him to sit down in the other chair which Tracy dragged up close to hers. Amanda looked away from the monitor whenever Tariq glanced in her direction but then returned to study it closely whenever he focused back on Tracy. One of the views showed Saeed was currently in heated conversation with another man, whom she assumed was Dhanial. With her enhanced hearing, she could hear them arguing back there but since she didn't understand Pashto, she could only guess Dhanial and the other three wanted to leave in the van.

Sure enough, the bay door in front of the van began to open and, moments later, the van headed out leaving Saeed standing there all alone. Amanda then watched the exterior views which showed the van leaving the warehouse and driving away.

Since she knew Saeed would be returning to the office, she quietly got up from the chair and strolled leisurely over to the area on the other side of the counter. She then looked out the window and, after a quick glance back at Tariq, asked in German, "How much longer before our tow truck gets here?"

Tracy had noted Amanda getting up and so she also stood up and followed after her. Tariq followed Tracy, of course, but answered Amanda by saying, "Maybe Saeed will know. He will be back soon."

Moments later, Saeed did return. He was very upset and, on being questioned about the tow truck, had nothing to say. Instead, he went over to the desk, picked up the telephone and called Talib. His day had now gone from complicated to totally screwed up.

Chapter Eleven
Mar 19, 2020

When the van with Dhanial and the others drove away from the warehouse, Jesse told Lieutenant Saunders to have one of his vehicles follow it, being careful to not be noticed. The lieutenant quickly made the call and the van was put under surveillance. Meanwhile, Jesse called Linda.

"We just spotted a van leaving from inside the warehouse. It's headed west, away from Leipzig. Lieutenant Saunders has some of his men following behind and they will keep us updated on where it goes."

"Any sign of the girls?" asked Linda.

"Not yet."

"I got a text from Tracy a few minutes ago. She said there were six men in there. Two were helping them and called Talib to arrange for a tow truck but the other four kept out of sight."

"I'm guessing Amanda was able to scent them," said Jesse. "Were they in that van?"

"Well, Amanda was able to scent they were hiding in one of the back rooms when she and Tracy went to use the restroom. But, Tracy said she heard Dhanial being mentioned as one of them. He's the guy Talib was worried about and sent Ravi to check on."

"Well, you told us how Ravi was now headed this way with five other guys." Jesse paused to consider things. Then he said, "Talib must have sent them here to stop Dhanial. I'll bet he's now in that van and headed somewhere to cause trouble."

"Assuming you're correct, Talib won't be happy. I'm starting to worry about the girls being caught in the middle of this. They might not be allowed to leave, even if their tow truck gets there before Ravi and the others arrive. How many armed men does Lieutenant Saunders have out there right now?"

"Well, in addition to him and the driver in this car, there's one other vehicle still here with four of his guys," answered Jesse. "Including me, that's seven. I'm sure we have plenty of firepower, if needed."

"Okay. Good to know. I've been keeping Colonel Schermerhorn in the loop. I know he's been in contact with someone in Germany's anti-terrorist group. Once we can confirm Talib and his men are holding any explosives, we can get the German authorities to move in. However, it might be necessary for you to act beforehand."

"Right. Understood. We're ready and can do that. It all depends on what Tracy and Amanda are finding out at this point."

When Saeed explained how Dhanial had left, headed for their target in Frankfurt with some bombing devices, Talib got really upset. Their conversation got very heated with Saeed on the defensive, claiming he'd not been able to stop anything, especially in front of the two women.

"What two women?" yelled Talib. "Wait … you mean the ones I called that tow truck for?" In his excitement, he'd almost forgotten about them. Suddenly, he got suspicious. "Are they still there?" He realized there had not been enough time yet for the tow truck to have arrived. "What do these women look like? Describe them to me."

Although Tracy and Amanda were with Tariq on the opposite side of the counter and a good distance from where Saeed was sitting, when Saeed's voice had risen that allowed Tracy to hear him describing her and Amanda. She left Tariq and moved closer toward Saeed, realizing the situation might suddenly be getting out of control. She grabbed her phone but kept it hidden.

Sure enough, after hanging up the phone, Saeed reached into one of the desk drawers and pulled out a handgun which he aimed at her. Then he yelled at Tariq to grab Amanda.

Recognizing it was time to call for help, Tracy dropped to the floor where Saeed couldn't see her and pulled out her phone. Amanda kept Tariq busy while Tracy quickly sent a text to John, signaling it was time for the Army guys to come to their rescue. Then she put her phone away, raised her hands, slowly stood up and faced Saeed. In Pashto, she asked, "What about our tow truck? Why are you holding a gun?"

Saeed was surprised at her speaking in Pashto but quickly answered, "Talib has cancelled your tow truck. He has instructed me to hold you both until he can get here. Come and sit down in one of these chairs." He waved his other hand at the two chairs in front of his desk.

Tracy glanced at Amanda and saw Tariq was now holding her arms and pushing her around the end of the counter, intent on forcing her towards a chair. With Saeed threatening them with his gun, she thought it best to play along until the reinforcements showed up. She followed behind Amanda but told her in English, "Let me know when I should make a distraction." She knew Amanda would sense when the guys were outside and ready to burst in.

Tariq pushed Amanda down into one of the chairs. Then he asked Saeed, "What's going on? What have they done?"

Saeed was staring at Tracy and said, "Talib thinks these women were at his store earlier today. They might be spying on us." He approached as Tracy took her seat in the other chair. Then, in Pashto, he yelled at her. "You can speak Pashto? How does a girl from Paris know our language? And, was that English just now?"

Tracy wanted to stall for time so she began talking, in Pashto. "I study languages at the university. But, we have done nothing wrong. My cousin and I stopped to buy some wine at a store in Leipzig today. This Talib person you speak of. Is he your boss? I think we met him at that store. Why does he accuse us of being spies? We have done nothing."

While she rambled on at the two men, she glanced around the office. She noted there were several sprinkler heads mounted in the ceiling, which was only eight feet high rather than the thirty feet typical out in the warehouse.

Just then, Amanda said in English, "Now would be good."

Tracy immediately created a small fireball just below four of the sprinkler heads near Saeed with more than enough heat to trigger each of them. As they began spraying water down, Saeed and Tariq were both caught by surprise. When the office door flew open and armed men rushed in, they were slow to react. Tracy and Amanda, meanwhile, dropped to the floor.

Before Saeed had a chance to fire his gun at anyone, he heard all the shouts from the intruders telling him to drop his weapon. Realizing he had no other option, he did so. Then, he and Tariq were forced to sit in the two chairs while others took charge of things.

Lieutenant Saunders yelled to one of his men, "Go shut off the water valve for all these sprinkler heads." Then he asked Tracy and Amanda, "Are you two ladies okay? We came as soon as we got your text."

Jesse could see the girls were fine. With a big grin, he said, "Lucky that sprinkler system suddenly decided to go off. I told the lieutenant not to wait for anything but to bust in here as soon as he could do so."

The sprinkler system soon was shut off and things quickly got sorted out. The office had been thoroughly drenched and was quite a mess. Fortunately, however, none of the electrical systems had shorted out. A couple guys began mopping and cleaning up.

Tracy gave the distributor rotor for her vehicle to one of the men to reinstall. However, they decided to leave the vehicle parked where it was with the hood still up since that was what Ravi would be expecting. The other two vehicles were then brought inside the warehouse behind the bay doors to get them out of sight.

Finally, after locking up Saeed and Tariq in one of the storerooms, they began a thorough search of the warehouse. When they opened the storeroom which Amanda had scented the odor of explosives coming from, sure enough, they found it contained several bombing devices along with plenty of materials and explosives to create even more. Plus, there were various weapons. Finally, they had the proof they needed.

They alerted Linda to have Lieutenant Colonel Schermerhorn put in a call for the German authorities. Then they waited for Ravi and the men he was bringing to arrive.

Ravi had only one of the five men with him while the other four were in the car right behind him. Since he was driving, he had the man with him accept the call coming in from Talib, telling him to put it on speakerphone. Then he answered, "Yes, Talib. This is Ravi."

"How far away are you?"

"Probably ten minutes, fifteen at the most. Why?" He could tell from Talib's tone that he was upset about something.

"Dhanial and those guys with him have already left. They loaded one of the vans with two of our bombing devices and are driving to Frankfurt. As you suggested earlier, they intend to bomb that nightclub we have next on our list."

"Do you want me to try to catch up with him? Or, maybe try to get to that nightclub before he does so I can stop him?"

"No, it's probably too late for that. Besides, Saeed tells me there are two women in his office right now. I want you to see if they might be the same ones who were in our store earlier today, right before I sent you to check on Dhanial. Remember the married couple? She had her cousin and the cousin's boyfriend with her."

Ravi was surprised to hear this and asked, "Why do you suspect they might be the same women? And, if they are, what about the husband and the boyfriend?"

"I've asked Saeed to hold them until you get there. I don't know where their men are. But, from the descriptions he gave me, I'm pretty sure they are the same women. They claim their car broke down and they needed a tow. I actually had called and arranged for that earlier but, after Saeed described them to me, I just now cancelled that tow truck. These women might be spies and … well … you know how worried I've been all week."

Yes, Ravi knew how paranoid Talib had been, ever since hearing about Candace Axtell and Oliver Bessom. He said, "Okay, I will check out these women. If they are spies, I'll let you know. You're still planning to come out here, right?"

"Yes, we need to all stay together right now. I have tried calling Dhanial but he doesn't answer. We need to listen to the news to learn if he does bomb that nightclub. Meanwhile, we will need to clear everything out of our warehouse and hide everyone at one of my safe houses until we know for sure about these spies and whether Dhanial succeeds or not."

"Okay, Talib. I will call you as soon as I'm at the warehouse and get a look at these two women. It should only be another five minutes or so."

Chapter Twelve
Mar 19, 2020

Upon Ravi's arrival, Lieutenant Saunders and his men quickly surrounded both cars. With weapons pointed at the occupants, the capture was without incident. In addition to being surprised, the men had not been armed and had no choice but to surrender. Ravi and all five of his men were brought inside to join Saeed and Tariq.

When Ravi spotted Tracy and Amanda, he began swearing in Pashto. Then, in German, he snarled, "Spies! Talib was right! You were at his store today. What's the meaning of this?" He hoped to feign innocence and somehow convince the men pointing guns at him that a mistake was being made.

Amanda answered in German, saying, "We have found the explosives which Talib has been storing here, Ravi. That evidence will prove Talib has been operating a terrorist cell and that you all are responsible for that bombing in Munich. These American soldiers will be turning you over to the German authorities."

Ravi responded with more curses, again in Pashto.

Tracy grinned and told John, "Wow, I'm learning *so* many new words today. I can't wait until I'm back at the academy and can share them with my classmates."

Just then, Gene and Oliver walked in. When they had gotten close to the warehouse, Linda had told them to stop and wait. She'd briefed them about the situation and the girls being rescued. Gene, of course, was greatly relieved that Amanda was okay. Then, after only a few minutes, Linda had told them they could continue and drive right up to the office, since Ravi and his men had now been arrested.

Amanda went over and told them how Tracy had created a diversion, setting off sprinkler heads, and how the Army guys had done an outstanding job, both rescuing them and then capturing Ravi and his men.

Oliver said, "Great! Sounds like things are under control. Talib and his other two men at the liquor store are being kept under surveillance by some of the men Lieutenant Saunders left behind. Candace doesn't really need guarding any longer, although two men are there, still doing that. And Linda told us the van which left here is under surveillance. Let's go check with Lieutenant Saunders for the latest on that."

They looked over and could see the lieutenant was briefing Jesse about something. They walked over but before they could ask any questions, Jesse announced, "We have a problem. The van which left here with explosive devices has managed to lose the tail we had on them. Lieutenant Saunders just heard from his guys. They're really sorry but, in staying back to avoid being noticed, they got snarled up in some traffic at two intersections. When they sped up on the road they thought the van had taken, they soon found they'd guessed wrong. They're backtracking now and will try taking another road but, with the lead the van now has on them, they're not sure they'll catch up. There were several possible routes and they'll only be guessing."

John and Tracy joined them and heard the bad news. Tracy said, "Oliver, let's ask Linda and Candy to go over to where these guys have been living and grab some of their personal things which you can use to track them. Remember how you and Millie helped search for those terrorists in Philadelphia? Using mattresses and blankets and stuff which Team Twenty-Two sent back from Afghanistan?"

Amanda said, "Good idea. I'll be able to identify which items contain the scent from Dhanial and the other three guys who were here and left in the van. Then, Oliver can follow whatever energy signature he can get from those items."

"Can Oliver do that from a helicopter?" asked Jesse. He was pretty sure he'd heard that finder witches could do that but wanted to make sure.

"Oh, yes," replied Oliver, nodding his head. "Can you get one for us? It will probably take more than an hour for Linda and Candy to break into those two apartments, round up enough items and then bring the stuff out here. If the Army can get a helo out here by then, we can maybe find that van before they get wherever they're going and blow up whatever their next target might be."

Jesse said, "I'm sure when Linda calls back to Colonel Schermerhorn and explains our plan, he'll manage getting some air support for us. Getting a helicopter here will definitely make a difference! Let's hope that can happen quickly enough."

Phone calls were made and those resulted in many more calls being made. But, twenty minutes later, Jesse got a call asking for information on where to land the Black Hawk helicopter which the Army was sending him and would arrive within the hour.

Talib meanwhile had decided he was in trouble. When he didn't hear from Ravi, he began making calls. After none of his calls to Ravi, Saeed or anyone else were answered, he realized the warehouse had to have been compromised. The two women must have been spies and until he could reach someone who could tell him differently, it was best to assume the worst. Instead of going out to the warehouse, he needed to go to his safe house instead.

He was worried about possible surveillance at his store, so he told Tabish and Musa they were locking up and leaving by way of the hidden exit which he had provided in anticipation that it might be needed someday. Once they had managed to leave and make their way to the safe house, making sure they weren't followed, he placed a call to Mullah Ahmed Kahtar.

After hearing what Talib had to report, Kahtar said, "You were right not to go out to that warehouse yourself. Is there anyone you can contact who might be able to check on things for you?" He knew Talib had developed various sources during the years he'd been in Germany.

"I plan on calling a few people who might help me with that," explained Talib. "But, if the authorities have gotten into my warehouse, they will have found the bombing devices. I'll need to leave Germany using my other identity, as will Tabish and Musa who are with me."

"Yes," agreed Kahtar. "If you can get to our safe house in France, I can then arrange for your safe return back here. What about the other members of your group? Can they get out?"

Talib said, "We will have to see whether Dhanial manages to succeed with our target in Frankfurt. That's probably the last opportunity anyone from my group will have here in Germany. If he contacts me after that, I'll tell him to go to France. He knows the plan for that. We will have to see what develops."

Dhanial looked again at the most recent text message he'd received from Talib. Unlike the earlier ones, demanding he return to the warehouse, this one was warning him not to do that. He wasn't sure whether to believe Talib that the authorities might have shown up there, arresting everyone and finding the rest of their explosives, but he wasn't calling him to learn more. No, Talib was furious about his taking the initiative and not waiting longer before attacking their target in Frankfurt. It would be time enough to call Talib *after* their attack. After their *successful* attack. That would make what he'd done acceptable.

And, if indeed the authorities had found the warehouse, as Talib was now suggesting? He would escape with his men to France. Let others worry about Oliver Bessom and whatever other demons might be chasing Talib or, perhaps, have already found him.

But, just to be certain he was not being followed, he had the driver turn down a side street and pull over. Again. He'd done this earlier. He knew how to evade possible surveillance and they had plenty of time to reach their target.

Chapter Thirteen
Mar 19, 2020

When William Gostoff got the call from his supervisor in Berlin, he was skeptical. But, nonetheless, he quickly assembled his Leipzig anti-terrorist team and brought them out to the warehouse at the address he'd been given. Allegedly, some American tourists and their U.S. Army security guards had located where the WIJO group responsible for the recent bombing in Munich was storing their explosives. Really?

Well, okay, the tourists and their bodyguards were the entourage with Candace Axtell, who had recently been on the news after visiting in Munich and then at the embassy. Yeah, he knew who she was. Who didn't? After all the publicity months earlier over her almost being beheaded by WIJO, the media the world over had made certain everyone knew who she was. Beautiful girl, important general's niece, dramatic last-minute rescue, big embarrassment for WIJO, etc., etc. Sure.

His supervisor claimed there were some American task force members in this entourage and so this Intel needed to be acted upon immediately. The Americans were holding eight suspected terrorists at the warehouse but others from the group were at large and another bombing attack might be happening in the next few hours. Hence, time was of the essence and it was his responsibility to get all this sorted out. Right away.

Wonderful. These Americans stir up a hornet's nest and now he's the one who would probably be getting stung.

On arrival at the warehouse, he asked for Linda Rayburn as soon as he entered the office. That was the name his supervisor gave him for the person on the American task force who had called this in. Her call had been to someone in the U.S. of course. That had led to his supervisor being pressured from whatever authorities in the German government those Americans had influenced. Since these were Americans, his question was in English, a language he fortunately was fluent in.

A young man stepped forward and said, "Ms. Rayburn will be here shortly."

"What about Candace Axtell?"

"She's with Ms. Rayburn."

"And you are?"

"I'm her fiancée, Oliver Bessom."

"You're Ms. Rayburn's fiancée?"

"No, Candace Axtell's."

"So, you were here when the suspects were detained?" asked Gostoff. He was not happy with any of this. He demanded, "I'd like to hear an explanation for what's going on here."

"Actually, no. I've just arrived. Gene Tremblay and I were following some of the terrorists to this warehouse. We arrived right after Lieutenant Saunders and his men apprehended them." Oliver had pointed first to Gene and then to the lieutenant while explaining this.

Gostoff was getting more and more frustrated with what he perceived as a run-around. Noting the American soldier apparently in charge was only a first lieutenant, his skepticism concerning everything grew. He again demanded, "Okay, I want to know exactly what happened here. Why was *anyone* apprehended? What was the evidence suggesting WIJO terrorists were involved?" He looked around at each of those gathered in front of him. His team members, meanwhile, had crowded into the office behind him but were waiting for him to provide instructions.

Tracy stepped forward and said, "Initially, we were acting on information obtained by our task force identifying Talib Mansoor as a terrorist. This was based on phone calls made to a WIJO leader in Afghanistan. Talib owns a liquor store in Leipzig which we … Oliver, Gene, Amanda and I … we visited there this morning."

"And, who are *you*?" asked Gostoff, startled that such a young girl was explaining things. He did not hide his exasperation.

"I'm Tracy McGonagle and the others brought me with them since I understand Pashto. When we were in Talib's liquor store, I overheard a conversation confirming the information we'd been given. Since our task force was able to locate this warehouse, operated by Talib, Amanda and I came out here to investigate." Pointing to Amanda, she continued, "She speaks

108

German. She and I pretended we had car trouble and came into this office and asked the two men in here for assistance."

Gostoff looked at Amanda, then Gene, then Oliver. "You are all members of an American task force?" His tone showed he was finding this incredulous.

"They are, but I'm not. They brought me along since I know Pashto."

Rolling his eyes, Gostoff asked, "Where did you learn Pashto? You don't look like someone from the Mid-East."

Tracy smiled and said, "At West Point. I'm a cadet there in my second year." Pointing to Captain Bonomo, she introduced him as one of the TAC Officers at the academy. Then she introduced John as her boyfriend. "We came to Germany this week with Candace Axtell hoping WIJO might react to her visit. That worked, since it was phone calls about her which our task force intercepted, enabling them to identify Talib."

"Why didn't your task force provide us with this information? Why would you Americans visit this warehouse without contacting us?" Gostoff was clearly annoyed.

"We had no concrete evidence. Only information which we realized the German authorities would not be able to act upon since it was merely verbal, without any documentation. That's why Amanda and I stopped in here. We hoped to find evidence which you could accept. And, we did. There's a room full of explosives back there which we believe you can match to what was used at that nightclub in Munich."

Not wanting to listen to this story any further without seeing this so-called evidence, he demanded, "All right. Let me see what you've found."

Two minutes later, he was looking at a room full of weapons, explosives and bombing devices which indeed represented significant evidence of unlawful activity. He'd have to have their lab which had examined the debris in Munich confirm there was a match to the explosives used there, but things were now looking much better. He might not be on some wild goose chase after all.

"Let me see your prisoners," asked Gostoff after he'd seen enough. He brought several members of his team with him to the room where Ravi and the others were being detained.

Ravi immediately began talking when Gostoff entered the room. "We are innocent. These Americans had no right to threaten us with weapons and lock us up in here. We have done nothing wrong. We don't know anything about what you've found in that other room. We're the victims here!"

Linda and Candace finally arrived, along with the Army guys escorting them. They had stopped at both apartments where the terrorists had been staying for the past several weeks. They scooped up blankets, sheets, pillows plus any other items which might contain residual energy. Candace was very familiar with what items Oliver might sense energy from with his supernatural ability. Then they'd continued to the warehouse where, thanks to the call from Captain Bonomo, they were aware of how Gostoff and his team had been handling things so far.

Gostoff came out to the office to meet them, leaving the eight terrorist prisoners for his team to take care of. He'd quickly tired of listening to Ravi's complaints and gave orders for the prisoners to be brought back to his office building in Leipzig where they'd be formally charged with various crimes, once all the evidence had been fully examined. He'd quickly realized none of them were ready to betray the others in their group and he wanted to learn what Linda Rayburn and her team might know. He'd been told there might be another bombing and wanted to get all the resources of his agency involved in stopping that, if at all possible.

After introductions were made, Linda said, "We're quite happy to let the German authorities take full credit for this arrest, Herr Gostoff. Our task force wishes to keep all aspects of our involvement secret, due to security reasons. Some of the tools and methods which were involved are highly classified, as I'm sure you will understand."

"Well, Tracy here did mention there were phone conversations between Talib Mansoor and some WIJO leader in Afghanistan," replied Gostoff. "And, my

111

supervisor says there might be another bombing attempt? What can you tell me about that?"

Linda nodded and said, "When Tracy and Amanda first arrived here, there were four other men besides Saeed and Tariq, the two you now have in custody. Ravi and the five men he brought arrived later. By that time, the van with those other four men had departed. Based on what Tracy heard before they realized she could understand Pashto, that van was headed out with bombing devices the men had loaded into it, with plans to attack their next target. Tonight."

"Why didn't Lieutenant Saunders and his men stop that van and arrest those terrorists as they were leaving here then?"

"At the time, it had not been established there were any explosives and bombing devices. Those were discovered after the lieutenant and his men rushed in to rescue the girls. Once they accomplished that … without any gunfire, by the way … well, then they discovered that room with the explosives during their subsequent search of the place."

Gostoff hadn't yet heard this part of the story and asked, "Why did Tracy and Amanda need to be rescued? And, how did the lieutenant know?"

"Saeed pulled a gun out and began threatening them," explained Linda. "Tracy sent a text to her boyfriend that help was needed. He was outside with the lieutenant and his men and they immediately reacted."

"Okay, I think I'm seeing this now. Of course, the fact that weapons and explosives were found is what makes all of this acceptable. Had there been nothing found, I'm not sure there was adequate justification for charging in here and subduing Saeed and Tariq. Why were they threatening the girls, anyway?"

Linda smiled and said, "Saeed was on the phone explaining to his boss, Talib Mansoor, about the four men leaving to attack their next target. Talib got suspicious about the girls being there and had Saeed describe them. Talib then recognized them from their visit to his store and insisted they be detained until Ravi got here. Ravi had been at his store during that visit and could confirm they'd been there. Talib was rightfully feeling worried about Candace Axtell's visit to Germany."

Gostoff looked at Tracy and nodded. He asked her, "You overheard enough to know you two were in trouble and somehow managed to text your boyfriend?" Then he chuckled. "I suppose things could have gone sideways and you women might have been hurt." When he saw Tracy's grin, acknowledging that, he said, "I think I'm missing some key elements in this story but that's okay." Looking back at Linda, he said, "What about the van that got away? Do you have a license plate number and description we can go with?"

"Yes, we do," said Linda, and she gave him that info. Then she added, "The lieutenant did have men in one of his vehicles following the van but, unfortunately, the van managed to lose them. His men were trying to avoid being noticed and got snarled up in traffic. The van was headed west but, who knows? It really could be anywhere by now."

"That's too bad. I'll have all our resources start searching for that van, based on this." Gostoff shook his head. "Without more to go on and not knowing their target? We might be too late."

Linda nodded and said, "We have a helicopter from the U.S. Army coming here. My team will try to circle around overhead and see if we can maybe spot them from the air. If we find them, I'll call you right away."

"Okay, any help like that will be appreciated," said Gostoff. He was finally satisfied these Americans were helping. "Meanwhile, my team will arrest Talib and any of his other guys back in Leipzig. Maybe we'll learn where the target might be from doing that. I doubt it but we need to try everything we can."

"Very well. Everyone on my team will be leaving when that helicopter gets here. I know you're taking these terrorists back with you. I assume you'll be taking all the weapons and explosives with you as well, right? For evidence?"

"Correct. We'll do a complete search but then we'll be leaving and taking everything with us. I don't see any need for anyone to stay and watch this place after that but we will be marking it as a crime scene."

Linda said goodbye and then she and her team went outside. The lieutenant's men had already opened up the bay doors and brought out the vehicles which they'd hidden earlier. They were ready to go and, except for the lieutenant, they would be leaving once the helo lifted off with Linda's team, taking all the vehicles they'd brought.

Lieutenant Saunders would go with Linda's team on the helicopter and provide direction to the men who'd gone ahead earlier and lost sight of the van. Hopefully, they'd be close enough to help once Oliver managed to locate where that van was located.

Chapter Fourteen
Mar 19, 2020

Gene and Amanda sorted through all the items which had been brought out from the terrorists' apartments. By the time the Army's Black Hawk helicopter arrived and touched down out in the parking lot, Amanda had identified those items which belonged to Dhanial and the three men who'd gone with him in the van. They separated these from all the other items and brought them to where Oliver was waiting with the rest of the team.

After examining them closely for a few moments, Oliver grinned and gave them all a thumbs up. He was able to clearly sense the residual energy from these men on the items and, with that signature to go with, he was able to sense the direction to where the men themselves were now. He knew he could follow that, just as Tracy had suggested and just as he had assured Jesse.

Captain Bonomo told Lieutenant Saunders, "Linda's task force includes the FBI's Psychic Division and Oliver is one of their best psychics. Linda and I will be giving our pilots direction to where we think the van might be, based on what Oliver is able to sense for us. That's highly classified and you must not include any reference to that in whatever reports you eventually file when this is all over. We won't be telling the pilots why we know where they need to fly. We'll merely tell them our source is classified. I'm pretty sure they already know this mission is top secret due to how it was arranged."

The lieutenant looked at Jesse with some skepticism but then nodded. He realized there were aspects to this entire mission he'd never understand but he was appreciative he'd been allowed to participate. It was all way over his head but he'd do his part. He checked in with Bravo-Three, the men he'd sent after the van, and advised them he'd be providing them with some guidance on where to look.

In addition to the two helo pilots, there were two crewmen; they waved Linda's team over and assisted them all with climbing aboard and getting seated and strapped in. Linda, Jesse and Lieutenant Saunders were provided with headsets and microphones enabling them to communicate with the pilots and crewmen. Once everyone was ready, the helicopter lifted off and climbed up to an altitude of a thousand meters.

Although it was now dark out, the pilots had helmet-mounted night vision goggles and could navigate anywhere they needed to go. When Oliver provided Jesse with a direction, he gave that to the pilots and they began their search. Glancing at the map which one of the crewmen gave Jesse, their direction was south-westerly and possibly toward Frankfurt. Lieutenant Saunders relayed that to Bravo-Three who then also headed off in that direction.

When the anti-terrorist team members Gostoff had sent to arrest Talib, Tabish and Musa finally broke into Talib's liquor store in Leipzig, they found it empty. Likewise, no one was home at any of the apartment addresses for these men. When all the vehicles registered to these men were also accounted for, it was obvious. The men had fled, probably to a safe house somewhere.

The German authorities were notified, an all-out search was initiated, photos were distributed, and checks were made at all public transportation centers. Every airport, train station, bus terminal and taxi company received notice these men were persons of interest whose whereabouts were to be reported immediately.

Searches made at the apartments turned up nothing helpful, in spite of obtaining the computers which had been left behind. When all resources had been exhausted with no immediate results, Gostoff placed a call back to Linda. He had finished up at the warehouse location and was returning to Leipzig at this point.

After Linda answered her phone, acknowledging she was still up in the helicopter and more than halfway to Frankfurt, Gostoff asked, "Are your sources still monitoring all phone calls from Talib Mansoor? I think you told me that was how your task force identified him in the first place, right?"

"Well, we will know if he uses his satellite phone to call back to Afghanistan. We might be able to provide a location if he does that but we never established any monitoring for other phone calls he or his men might be making. Why? Wasn't he at his liquor store?" Linda had not yet heard any reports from the men Lieutenant Saunders had left doing surveillance.

"No, it looks like he and his men have gone to ground," answered Gostoff. "They're not using any of their known vehicles or prior locations ... we doubt they're coming out to the warehouse. I still have people there but, if he was nervous about Ms. Axtell's visit like you said and wasn't able to reach Ravi or Saeed after they were arrested?"

"Right. I understand," agreed Linda. "Okay. I'll let my people know. If they learn anything, I'll get back to you."

"Thanks." After a short pause, Gostoff asked, "You say you're checking for that van out near Frankfurt?"

"It's only a guess but, yes. If we locate the van, I will let you know right away."

They said their goodbyes and disconnected.

Linda asked Lieutenant Saunders to check and, after he conferred with his surveillance team at the store, he confirmed what Gostoff had told her. They never saw anyone leave the store but did notice Gostoff's men rush in. They were guessing there must have been a hidden exit since it was obvious no arrests had been made.

Linda then let the others know Talib had managed to escape. But that situation would have to wait … they needed to focus on finding Dhanial and that van with the explosive devices first.

Ten minutes later, Oliver said, "I think we may be getting close now. I'm sensing stronger signals and those are coming from somewhere below rather than from up ahead. Let's have the pilot circle around to the right and take us down a little lower."

Amanda and Jesse were seated next to a window on the left side of the aircraft while Tracy, John and Lieutenant Saunders were seated next to one on the right. They'd been the ones to see the van back at the warehouse earlier and hoped they could recognize it again once they got somewhere near, even though it was now dark out.

There were two main routes from Leipzig into Frankfurt and they were now over one of them, not far from Giessen. They'd been guiding Bravo-Three who were only about fifteen minutes back, having been speeding as fast as possible. As they descended lower, there were enough lights allowing them to determine what vehicles were travelling on the various roadways.

John asked Tracy, "Isn't that the van we want? See the one which just went through that intersection?" He was pointing so she could see.

"Yes!" exclaimed Tracy. "That's the one!" She and John pointed so the others could see and Jesse came over to look. He alerted the pilots they had a suspect vehicle down below and described it for them, asking that they circle overhead but stay far enough away so it wouldn't be obvious they were following this van.

Lieutenant Saunders was very impressed. Somehow … and, he knew he'd never know just how … Oliver and Linda's team had indeed managed to locate the van. As their aircraft circled lazily overhead, he was able to see it well enough to satisfy himself they really had the right vehicle. When they checked the license plate number which appeared in one of the photos the co-pilot managed taking, it checked. They had the correct van.

After checking with Bravo-Three, it was confirmed they were only about ten minutes away. If the target was in Frankfurt, which they had been guessing for a while now, it looked possible to intercept the van before it reached there. Linda gave Gostoff a call to ask that he get his organization to take the lead. She wanted Bravo-Three to only play a supporting role which, hopefully, wouldn't be needed.

Gostoff had just reached Leipzig when Linda called. He hadn't given her chances of locating that van much hope but, on learning she was now circling overhead and had confirmed the license plate, he promised to get someone from the Frankfurt anti-terrorist group in touch with her right away.

He had been keeping his supervisor in Berlin up to date with all the developments and, after getting Linda's call, he quickly passed along her request.

More calls were made and it didn't take long before one Jordan Dietrich in Frankfurt was told to call

Linda Rayburn and provide all necessary resources in stopping the van and arresting the suspected terrorists. Detailed info was provided on the types of explosives and bombing devices, along with possible weapons, which might be in that van.

Dietrich called Linda to get the story firsthand and promised he'd scramble a team to intercept the van. They discussed possible locations where a blockade might be set up, but they needed to see which route into Frankfurt the van would take before any decision could be made. When Linda advised the van had just left Route 5 and was now on Route 661, Dietrich stated he wanted to stop them just before the Preungesheim district, on the northern outskirts of Frankfurt.

Linda told Dietrich, "Our Bravo-Three team is in a vehicle now only five minutes behind the van. It will be in position to stop any retreat the van might attempt. Wait one … we need to check something with our pilot."

Jesse had been signaling her, pointing at his watch and at the pilot. She switched over to use her headset to communicate with the pilot and learned they could stay on station for at least thirty minutes. On the phone again to Dietrich, she added, "We'll be up here for another half hour or so. Then we'll need to refuel."

Dhanial was pleased. He was confident this attack would go just as well as the one they'd done in Munich, only better since they were placing two bombing devices. He'd go into the club first, checking things out. Then two of his guys would come in through the back door he'd open for them, while his remaining guy stayed with the van, ready for a quick getaway. They had done a thorough surveillance of this particular club's layout ten days earlier; he'd have no problem taking out the one security guard in the back and letting his guys sneak in.

Once they each had placed their explosives under tables near support columns, like they'd managed doing in Munich, they all could make their way back out and climb into the van. After they were well clear, they'd detonate their bombs remotely. Boom! Another big moment for WIJO with a strong message sent to the rest of the world. He was sure this would really enable him to move higher up in WIJO's organization.

They'd taken a leisurely route so far, making sure they were not being followed and driving at a normal pace. Now they were only minutes away from their destination and the timing would be just right. He looked ahead along the stretch of highway and …

Suddenly, there were flashing lights up there! Oh, oh! What was this?

"Hey, it looks like police are looking for someone," he yelled. "Pull over and stop. Let's see what happens. If any of them come toward us, we need to turn around and go the other way. We cannot allow our van to be stopped and searched."

Chapter Fifteen
Mar 19, 2020

Tracy watched as the van pulled to a stop. There were several vehicles now racing towards the van, lights flashing, forcing traffic to pull over to one side or the other. Then she saw the van start back up, veering across the road and crossing to the opposite lane. It was obvious it planned to make a run for it.

She focused on the front of the van, where the engine was. She didn't need to extend her arm, really. She aimed with one finger and was able to control the energy which she'd been gathering. Suddenly a bright fireball burst, going right through the van's hood and into its engine compartment. The van ground to a halt. It wasn't going anywhere after that.

Men came scrambling out, waving weapons. The vehicles with the flashing lights quickly pulled to a stop nearby. Doors opened and men with weapons climbed out, using the open doors for protection. Shots were fired and in just moments, it was over. The four men from the van were all down. Then the police rushed towards the van with fire extinguishers. Fortunately, before the fire had spread to anywhere inside the van, where the explosives were located, it was put out.

It would be learned that two men from the van were killed while Dhanial and one other were badly wounded. They would survive, however, and be able to stand trial with Ravi and the others later. Two of the anti-terrorist team members were wounded, but only with superficial wounds. The arrest was considered a huge success.

Bravo-Three arrived shortly after it was over. They asked for Jordan Dietrich but since he was back at headquarters, they merely talked to him on the phone. They did, however, get to see firsthand how everything had played out. Like everyone else on site, they found no explanation for the mysterious explosion which caused the van's engine to burst into flames. That never would be explained and would be written up as a strange anomaly. A *lucky* strange anomaly, of course, since had the van not stopped when it did, there might have been some collateral damage.

In hindsight, having the anti-terrorist forces and police all flashing their lights the way they'd done might not have been the best strategy. As explanation, since no one was making any excuses, there had been very little time for these Frankfort teams to react. Once there was one vehicle flashing its lights, that quickly resulted in all the others doing so as well. But all had ended well, so … like the strange fire anomaly … not much was said about it. The contents of the van got all the attention. A bombing attack by WIJO terrorists had definitely been stopped, with the men responsible for planning that arrested. The authorities would have no difficulty in proving these men were responsible for the attack in Munich as well.

Linda and her team had only circled overhead for a few minutes after seeing how events unfolded down below. Then they'd headed off to an airport nearby to refuel.

Linda talked to both Dietrich and Gostoff, congratulating them for a successful operation and received their thanks for the behind the scenes assistance her team had provided. Then she called Lieutenant Colonel Schermerhorm and briefed him on everything.

Once her phone calls were over, she rejoined the others on her team who had somehow managed getting several pizzas delivered. For this impromptu pizza party, they were able to use a hangar which had been made available to them, thanks to calls their pilots had made. It was nice to know people who knew people. They were all in a very up mood.

Away from being overheard by those not on her team, Linda explained what was left for them to still accomplish. "I asked if we could keep our Army helicopter for another day and Colonel Schermerhorm said he was confident he could make that happen. We already have Lieutenant Saunders and his guys, of course. We'll return to Leipzig tonight and get some rest at our hotel. In the morning, we'll let Oliver take us to wherever Talib is hiding with his two men."

Oliver grinned and said, "I was hoping you'd say that! If we still have that helo, it won't be any problem to locate those guys. Then, you can have the lieutenant and his men apprehend them. Or, will you be inviting Gostoff to do that?"

"No, we'll let Jesse and Lieutenant Saunders do the apprehending. They did such an outstanding job rescuing Tracy and Amanda, I'm sure they'll be quite capable of capturing Talib and whomever else he has with him. Then? We'll have to see what our task force back home wants us to do. They'll be conferencing all night on that while we're getting our rest. The consensus back home is to use this opportunity to send our own message to WIJO. Having Missy right there in Afghanistan where she can help get our message across just makes this an ideal occasion for doing exactly that."

There were several calls of, "Hear, hear!" and "Okay, now! Let's go!" The enthusiasm was plentiful and, when their pilot approached and announced he'd just received word that he was to provide Linda and her team with continued support for another twenty-four hours, that was met with further cheers.

Thus, it was a happy team which climbed back aboard the Black Hawk for a return flight to Leipzig. Lieutenant Saunders called ahead and arranged for a couple more rooms for the pilots and their crew at the same hotel where everyone else was staying. And, of course, he had vehicles waiting when they landed to take them all back to that hotel.

Oliver and Candy went to their room where Candy insisted on showing Oliver just how much she appreciated his outstanding wizardry in finding that van. Their passionate lovemaking was a very strong incentive for Oliver to find those remaining terrorists in the morning. Their decision to come along on this mission,

127

hopefully stirring up those WIJO terrorists and getting them to reveal themselves, had definitely been a good one. They both drifted off to sleep, eventually, feeling very good about things.

Gene and Amanda were also super excited about having come on this trip to Germany. It had been their idea for Oliver and Candace's embassy visit to be here. Not only had Amanda been able to reunite with her family, introducing Gene, but their mission to obtain justice for Johan and Justine was clearly a huge success. They were certain Oliver would locate the remaining terrorists and, from what Linda was saying, the task force they worked for was still planning something.

Jesse and Linda were finding they couldn't wait to climb into bed and make love. They each had learned a lot that day about the other person and it reinforced all the feelings they'd found about each other in Berlin. They were finding there were real depths to those feelings. The fire kindled during their first few nights together was now blazing strongly and they were more comfortable with being together than either had ever dreamed possible. They didn't need to look ahead to what the future might be bringing. They just knew they'd somehow manage to continue their relationship long term and, for right now? They were enjoying themselves tremendously. It was a long time before their passionate lovemaking gave way to their falling asleep, still twined together in loving embraces.

And, what about Tracy and John?

"That laser firebolt was very impressive," said John as he began undressing for bed. "I didn't notice any energy being drained from me when you blasted that van. I'm guessing you stored up enough energy beforehand and didn't need to draw much, if any, from the rest of us when you did that, right?" He chuckled.

Tracy grinned and said, "I did gather some energy from everyone while we were flying along, but you're right ... I didn't need all that much." She had been removing her clothes and tossing them helter-skelter and was down to just her bra and panties.

"Oh, why not? Are you the Everready Energizer Bunny now?" He was still only half undressed and paused to admire the way she was now parading around, teasing him in her skimpy, sexy lingerie.

"Actually, that might be a good analogy," murmured Tracy as she came over, pushed him back so he sat down on the bed and then she helped him remove one of his shoes. "You do realize the Spring Equinox is tomorrow and my highly developed witchy powers always escalate at such times, right?"

"Ahhh, yes! That's right! You being such an extraordinarily powerful witch, your magic knows no bounds whenever any of the eight points in the year's cycle are reached. And, with this ... what? The Vernal Equinox? When the planets are aligned? When the

129

daytime and nighttime have the same length? This really amps you up!"

"You know it's *not* magic, John! The supernatural ability those Fabulous Fates have gifted me with … the power with limits *unleashed* when I bonded with *you* …", she yanked his pants and underwear down and off, throwing them over her shoulder, "is way beyond any mere magic." She straddled him, grinding her wet panties on his exposed manhood, thrilled at how hard that was rapidly getting.

John groaned and said, "I know you get insatiably *horny* during these *magical* moments." He removed her bra and flung that in the same direction his pants had gone. Then, latching his mouth onto one of her prominent nipples, now pebbled and very aroused, he mumbled, "MmmMmmm!" as he began sucking.

They continued to play and Tracy's lusty libido did prove to be quite difficult to satisfy. Of course, John loved all the hard work that required, giving her three very intense orgasms so she was finally limp and satiated. They both then slept for several hours.

Tracy did wake up, however, and … yes, she was still needy … so she woke John up and insisted on even more attention.

However, it only required one orgasm to satisfy her that time.

Chapter Sixteen
Friday, Mar 20, 2020

After breakfast, Linda again assembled her team and called into Robert's team. They were crowded into her room and she put the call on speakerphone so they all could participate. After they got through with all the greetings, she got right to the purpose of the call. "What does everyone want us to do today? We're going to have Oliver find Talib and then we'll have Lieutenant Saunders capture him and his two guys. But Dale was saying last night how this was an opportunity to send a message. So, I'm guessing we don't simply turn them over to the German authorities."

Dale said, "You can do that at the end of the day. But, since you have that helicopter available, we think you should transport them down to Regensburg for a little visit with Amanda's pack. That's assuming she can talk her former pack into agreeing to participate and *not* merely kill them. We're looking for Oliver to orchestrate a confrontation with wolves and, using his demonic ability of course, control them."

"I think I can convince Klauss, their Alpha, to go along," said Amanda. "The rest of the pack will do whatever he says. I know they'll enjoy the opportunity to face the men responsible for killing Johan and Justine. But, tell us more about what you have in mind."

Lieutenant Colonel Schermerhorm said, "We want you to make a video which you can stream live to a website Marie has set up. Missy will share that video in real time with Mullah Ahmed Kahtar in Afghanistan and have him on the line with you so he can interact. Oliver will threaten to have his wolves ... his *hellhounds*, actually ... attack and eat Kahtar's men right before his very eyes."

Amanda exclaimed with glee, "Oh, yes! Klauss will like this plan."

"After Oliver and Missy get Kahtar to understand what can happen to any future WIJO terrorists, Oliver will spare these three. The point will have been made that our demons can and will punish WIJO, anytime and anywhere. Since Missy will be confronting Kahtar in his own home ... well, we think he'll get the message. And, we'll have copies of the video sent to Aziz and Mohammad Nabir as well."

They discussed details of the plan for several minutes and then hung up so Amanda could call Klauss. She obtained his enthusiastic support and learned where he wanted them to land their helicopter, once they had the three terrorists captured. Then, they all went out to get started with the plan.

Linda, Oliver, Tracy and John went with their helicopter pilots and crew members out to the airport while the others climbed into vehicles with Lieutenant Saunders and his team. They believed Talib was still somewhere in the Leipzig area since Oliver could sense their energy was providing strong signatures.

Linda explained to the pilots how Oliver's psychic ability might help them locate more terrorists and off they went. Based on the directions Oliver provided, the helicopter triangulated an area on the outskirts of the city and, when the vehicles with Lieutenant Saunders and the others were less than a mile away, it landed in a nearby field. The vehicles met them there.

Oliver then joined the others and led them to what looked like an abandoned farmhouse. He assured Jesse he could sense all three men were in there. Jesse then talked to Lieutenant Saunders and, after a brief recon, they decided on an assault plan.

This farmhouse was supposed to be a safe house, where Talib and whomever he brought with him could hide. It was not really a place which could be defended from any assault and did not have much in the way of sensors or security. When the lieutenant and his men barged in, going through all entrances at the same time, they were able to catch Talib, Tabish and Musa completely by surprise. Musa did attempt pulling a weapon out but was wounded in the arm when he didn't drop it fast enough. It was all over in just a few minutes and the only shot fired was the one which wounded Musa.

Once the three terrorists were disarmed and handcuffed, Linda and her team came in and confronted them. Talib recognized Candace as well as the four who had been in his liquor store the day before. He began cursing, in Pashto.

Speaking in Pashto as well, Tracy said, "We believe everyone in your group has now been captured. However, we want to make certain of that. I see you know who Candace Axtell is." After gesturing towards

Candy, she then pointed to Oliver. "Let me introduce her fiancée, Oliver Bessom. Do you know who he is as well?"

After more curses, Talib said, "Yes, he is a demon! I know all about him. But I did not recognize him in my store yesterday and that is why you have captured me."

Tracy looked at Jesse and said, "It might be best if the lieutenant and his men wait outside. Besides, they need to bring their vehicles up closer to take us all back to where our helicopter is waiting, right?"

Lieutenant Saunders understood and didn't need Jesse or Linda to say anything. He immediately gave orders to his men and they promptly left so only Linda's team was still inside with their captives.

Turning back to Talib and again speaking in Pashto, Tracy said, "The German authorities have found all the explosives you were keeping at your warehouse. That evidence will tie all of you to the WIJO bombing attack in Munich. Oliver wants to determine whether there is anyone else in your group who might not have been captured yet. You do know we stopped Dhanial last night, right?"

Talib had seen that on the news and immediately he began cursing again. Finally, he said, "I know two of my employees were killed last night. Everyone else has been arrested. I don't know anything about explosives or WIJO attacks."

Tracy translated Talib's comment to the others. Then she asked Oliver to say a few words about their plan. She didn't know if any of these men understood English, but if they did, she wanted them to hear it from Oliver.

"We don't plan on turning you over to the authorities," said Oliver. "We are taking you for a helicopter ride instead to where some of my hellhounds are waiting. We will let them determine whether you are WIJO terrorists and if you will tell us the truth about things."

Tracy translated Oliver's announcement, with emphasis on the hellhounds he was threatening them with. Naturally, that was met with more cursing from all three men. Then Talib, Tabish and Musa were blindfolded and led outside to the vehicles which had been brought up. Musa's arm had been bandaged and, although it was painful, he was in no immediate danger. The bullet had gone through and the bleeding had stopped.

Amanda called her parents who were anxiously waiting with Klauss. She explained things had gone as planned and they were returning to their helicopter with their three captives. Linda made a similar call to Robert's team.

Twenty minutes later, Linda and her team were airborne in the Black Hawk. They'd said goodbye to Lieutenant Saunders, explaining they'd let him know when they'd be returning to the airport but that it wouldn't be until much later that day. The blindfolds were kept on their prisoners to prevent them from knowing where they were going and to heighten their discomfort. It was on to Regensburg and the next phase of their plan.

Les told Ed Collingsworth that, according to Mike, Missy was now at Mullah Ahmed Kahtar's home and ready to materialize once Mike gave her the signal. "She's located one of his white tunics which she plans to wear, once she materializes."

Many on Robert's team were gathered back at their Hanscom AFB conference room, anxiously waiting for further word from their Germany team. Everyone was logged into the website Marie had established, ready for the show to begin.

Ed asked, "Is he alone or will she have to knock out a few of his terrorist buddies once this gets started?"

"He's alone. She was prepared to disable anyone else, like you're suggesting, but it doesn't look like that will be needed."

Dale Hewson chuckled and said, "We all know how good Missy is at multi-tasking. She'll handle things on her end, regardless of what comes up. Let's hope Linda and Oliver are able to manage everything on their end."

"Will Gene and Amanda be joining the pack and participating as wolves?" asked Marsha. "And, what about Tracy? Will she be doing anything?"

Lieutenant Colonel Schermerhorn said, "I can see you folks in Kabul are thinking along the same lines we are back here. Yes, Gene and Amanda were thrilled when Klauss said they could join in the fun and run as wolves. And Tracy agreed to create several fireballs which the wolves will be racing out underneath of when they first make their appearance. When Oliver calls for his hellhounds, it should look as though all hell is breaking loose."

"Mike? We just got Linda's text. Go ahead and give Missy the signal now. Let us know when she has Kahtar's computer logged into our website and is ready for all hell to break out."

When Missy got Mike's signal, she Shifted to her human form, grabbed the garment she'd selected from Kahtar's bedroom closet, slipped that on, and then went out to the living room where Kahtar was watching the news on TV. She made his television set disintegrate into thousands of little pieces, getting his attention immediately, and in Pashto said, "Mullah Ahmed Kahtar! Although we have not met before, I think you probably know who I am."

After getting over his initial shock at her dramatic entrance into the room, he tried to jump up from his chair but found there was a strange force pushing against his chest, preventing him from doing that. He recognized her, of course. Since she'd spoken in Pashto, he did as well, saying, "Missy McCrea. One of the demons from the United States which I have heard so much about. Are you here to murder me?"

Continuing in Pashto, she said, "No, no! Far from it, this visit. But, if I need to make any return visits, that very well might happen. No, I'm here today because I want to show you what is happening to your terrorist cell in Germany." She knew where he had placed his phone as well as his laptop computer, which was over on a desk in his office. She used her telekinesis ability to bring both items floating into the room. She set them down on a table which she then made slide across the room so it was in front of Kahtar.

Kahtar said, "I learned today that many of those holy followers of Allah have been illegally arrested by the German authorities. Am I correct that you and Oliver Bessom are somehow responsible for this?"

Missy had booted up the laptop and was now logging into Marie's website. She let Mike know and then waited a few moments. Then she said, "I will let you speak directly to Oliver … I'm dialing his phone number right now. He only speaks English but … here he is!" After putting the phone on speakerphone, she put it down on the table and turned the laptop so Kahtar could see its screen. Switching to English, she said, "Oliver? Do we have a good connection? I'm here with Mullah Ahmed Kahtar."

On the screen, Oliver Bessom and Candace Axtell could be seen. They were standing behind three men who were kneeling. The men on their knees wore handcuffs and blindfolds. It was obvious they were helpless. Oliver removed the blindfolds and Kahtar was very surprised to recognize Talib Mansoor. He did not recognize the others but assumed they were two of Talib's men.

In English, Oliver said, "Hi, Missy! I'm glad you're available since you can translate for me. We have Talib, Musa and Tabish with us but they have not understood any of my questions. I'm putting you on speakerphone." He waved with the hand in which he was holding his phone, then handed that to Candy. "My questions are concerning the terrorist group he's been leading over here. We think these are the last three not yet arrested for that WIJO bombing in Munich but we want to be certain."

Missy first translated what Oliver had said to Kahtar and then she continued in Pashto, saying, "Talib? Have my friends Oliver and Candace explained to you about our hellhounds yet? We like to use them when we want to get the truth."

Chapter Seventeen
Mar 20, 2020

Talib had been looking around ever since the blindfold had finally been removed. He knew he'd been taken in a helicopter to some remote location but had no idea where it was. The flight had been more than an hour. Then, he'd been brought out into what he could now see was a huge clearing, surrounded by trees. He'd been told Missy McCrea would be calling and that she would have Kahtar with her. Apparently, all of his worst fears had indeed come true. Hearing her speak about hellhounds only added to those fears. He said nothing.

Linda was filming this while Tracy, John and Jesse remained out of sight from her camera. When Missy stopped speaking in Pashto, Linda waited for a few moments. None of their captives seemed willing to say anything so she gave Tracy the signal to begin.

Tracy had John and Jesse in a circle with her but really didn't need to draw energy from them. She was bursting with power and extended both arms out, pointing toward the far tree line across the clearing and creating a dozen fireballs, maintaining them about six feet off the ground. Then she added a dozen more. And, more after that.

Linda shifted the camera's view so it was focused on all the fireballs which had suddenly appeared. Then, from beneath what now looked like a wall of flames, animals began appearing. More and more wolves came racing forward, rushing right at the three men kneeling in the midst of the clearing. The screams of terror from the men were drowned out by all the howling which these wolves were doing.

Talib, Tabish and Musa tried to stand, wanting to get away, but since their legs had been tied together and to one another, their mad scrambling only resulted in them all sprawling on the ground instead. The animals seemed to ignore Oliver and Candace while snarling, snapping their fangs, and surrounding the three captives. Just when it appeared their throats would be ripped out, Oliver said something to the beasts and at the last moment they stilled and quieted down. It was obvious he was somehow controlling them.

Oliver said, "Missy, will you ask these men about any others in their group who might still be at large? Or, have we truly captured all of the men responsible for the WIJO attack?" In the background, the fireballs had somehow diminished, with many going out completely.

Missy translated Oliver's request and, looking at Kahtar, she spoke to him next. "Please order Talib to answer truthfully. Otherwise, our hellhounds are ready to devour him and his men."

Kahtar was very shaken by the whole scene he'd watched play out before him. He had believed Missy and Oliver were demons before this. He knew they had great powers. But he never imagined they could do all this. Come into his home? Force him to witness what surely was something coming right from hell? He said,

"Talib, speak quickly and speak the truth! Are there any members in your group not yet arrested?"

Talib recognized Kahtar's voice and could see no reason not to answer. He shouted, "No, there is no one! No one! Everyone has been arrested or killed. We three are the last ones remaining. Please ... be merciful ... turn us over to the German authorities!"

Missy translated this for Oliver but then went on, in Pashto, "WIJO has not shown any mercy. Why should we?" The wolves, meanwhile, continued to threaten. They were very convincing as they circled around the men, snarling and baring their fangs. Unless Oliver stopped them, they were quite clearly going to kill these men, tearing them limb from limb. The ravenous behavior they were showing was totally convincing.

But then Oliver looked into the camera and said, "This time, we will show mercy." He gestured to the wolves and they reluctantly backed away. He motioned for them to go and slowly, they began returning to where they'd started from. Looking back into the camera, he said, "WIJO must stop all attacks. Otherwise, we will come for the leaders next. We know who you are. We know where you are. We cannot be stopped."

Missy translated Oliver's words and added some of her own. "Oliver will give your three terrorists to the German authorities. They will stand trial for their crimes and be punished. But, as I did in England, we want to further demonstrate the power we demons wield. We therefore will send lightning bolts down today. We will send them down to incinerate the warehouse near

142

Leipzig where your weapons and explosives were being stored. All of the inventory belonging to the liquor business which Talib was running for WIJO will be destroyed. This is our last warning. And, these are but small examples of what power we can bring against WIJO. We can find and destroy all of you as well as all the sources WIJO has for wealth here in the Mid-East, just as we've done in the U.S., England and Germany."

Missy then shutdown the laptop and destroyed the phone, melting it with a small fireball. When that went out, she looked over at Kahtar who was cringing in fear. "Don't make me come back. I promise you will not survive my return. Nor will Shahid Omar Aziz or Mohammad Nabir. Be sure to tell them that."

Then, in a shimmer of light, she vanished. As the white tunic she'd been wearing drifted down to the floor, Kahtar was finally able to move forward. Slowly, he rose from his chair. He stared at where his phone had been and then at the remnants of his TV. Using his laptop which was still functional, he placed a video call to Aziz.

Missy returned to where Mike, Les and Marsha were still on their conference call with Robert's team. She had quickly dressed after Shifting back to her human form in the bedroom. "Hey? How did everyone like the show? I thought our team in Germany did a really great job!" She had especially enjoyed the way Tracy's wall of flames had looked. It had indeed given the impression that the wolves were hellhounds, bursting forth from the fires of hell.

Lieutenant Colonel Schermerhorn said, "We all thought that was epic! We will provide copies to all the WIJO leaders, using Kahtar's own email account to send it."

"I added that part about the warehouse being destroyed," said Missy. "That little embellishment you folks suggested ought to make Tracy very happy. You're certain there aren't any people there to be in the way?"

"Yes, we checked with the German authorities. They removed all the evidence and the place should be abandoned now. Of course, Gene and Amanda will be able to scent if anyone is nearby before Tracy starts unleashing any of her lightning bolts."

"Excellent! It looks like our work is done here. I'll spend the day checking on how the other WIJO leaders are reacting to all this. Then, tomorrow morning we can fly to Berlin. It will be nice to join the others for some actual vacation time. We can then return home the day after that."

Linda's team had their Black Hawk pilots fly them back to Talib's warehouse outside Leipzig, where they had first met them. Since they didn't want the pilots or crew to witness the actual warehouse destruction, they asked to be dropped off and left alone for two hours. They exited the helicopter, bringing their three blindfolded captives with them, and watched as the aircraft lifted back up and climbed away.

Oliver asked Tracy to translate for him. Then he confronted Talib, Tabish and Musa. Yanking their blindfolds off, he said, "Now you will bear witness to the destruction of your warehouse, just as we promised."

Tracy translated and then stepped away, with John, Jesse, Gene and Amanda. She put them in a circle with her while Linda stayed back, again filming things. Candace stood next to Oliver, who was being watched closely by their three captives. Gene gave her the thumbs up, so she began to draw power and energy from all around.

Oliver extended his arm to the sky, pretending to be the one calling for lightning, and Tracy began sending down bolt after bolt of destructive fire, each one cracking with a thunderous roar immediately after. She was able to really get into this, drawing and expending tremendous amounts of energy ... possibly more than she'd ever done before. Yes! Each time she exercised her power this way, her capability seemed to expand and her awareness grew. It was awesome!

Talib and his guys thought Oliver was the one doing all this, of course. They watched in fear and trepidation as the damaging lightning bolts caused a raging fire, fueled by all the liquor inside the burning warehouse. How was this possible? It was obvious to them that Oliver was indeed a terrible demon.

By the time the Black Hawk returned for them, the warehouse was mostly a pile of smoking rubble.

They boarded the aircraft and ignored the questioning looks from the pilots and crew. Some things would have to remain a mystery. And, highly classified of course. The helicopter lifted back up and brought them back to the airfield at Leipzig where Lieutenant Saunders and his men were waiting. Linda thanked the pilots and crew members for their fabulous support and assured them their superiors would be getting a letter, praising them.

Then, getting directions from Gostoff to where his headquarters was located, they delivered their three WIJO terrorist prisoners. Gostoff wanted to know how they had managed to locate Talib and his men. He also wanted answers to many other questions, but Linda simply smiled and said, "You should ask Talib."

"I will need to hear from *you*," Gostoff blustered. "For my report!"

"Sorry! We did confirm that all of the WIJO terrorists are now in your custody. Your organization can take full credit for that. As for any crazy stories which Talib, Tabish and Musa might be telling? I'm sure you will find those are not credible and not worth investigating."

They all said goodbye and then returned to their hotel. It had been a full day but one that was very satisfying.

Epilogue

Sunday, Mar 22, 2020

The return flight back to New York was uneventful, although there was definitely a party atmosphere amongst those aboard. And, they had Missy with them. She was able to provide interesting anecdotes concerning each of the WIJO leaders and how they were now definitely convinced to stand down. At least for the near future.

They had all reunited the day before, Linda's team returning with Lieutenant Saunders and his men in their vehicles, driving up from Leipzig, and checking back into the VIP housing near the Clay Atlee building. Missy, Mike, Les, Marsha and Sergeant Town had flown in the "P" Branch jet from Kabul and, with their two pilots, checked into rooms at the same housing facility. Calls had been made, arranging things for them all, and they enjoyed a very nice luncheon in the VIP mess hall.

Then, they'd toured Berlin. Lieutenant Saunders had his security force escort them in small groups, each going to see what interested them most and find places to eat where they could boast about how delicious the German food was. And, the German beer, of course. Did they manage to crowd into one day, evening and night all the excitement of a week's spring break vacation? Well … they tried!

And, after breakfast that morning, saying goodbye at the airport to Lieutenant Saunders and his men was bittersweet. Linda promised their superiors would also be receiving letters of praise for every person who had helped them that week.

This time, before most dozed off in their plush seats, it was Gene and Amanda who were entertaining Sergeant Town with descriptions of the fires and lightning bolts they'd experienced Tracy tossing around.

Amanda said, "When Gene and I rushed out under Tracy's wall of fire with my former pack and charged those three terrorists responsible for killing Johan and Justine? We truly felt as though we were being unleashed as hellhounds and we'll never forget how wonderful that was!"

Linda assured the sergeant she had it all on video and would make certain he got a copy. So would Amanda's pack, of course. It would always be a special memory for them.

On arrival at JFK airport, there again were those leaving while others were continuing on up to Boston. Missy, Tracy, Jesse and Sergeant Town were all returning to West Point. The sergeant wanted someone to make a video of the goodbye kisses which Missy was giving Mike and which Tracy was giving John. Linda was busy kissing Jesse, however, so was not available to do that. He grumbled good naturedly and then took out his smart phone and made the video himself.

As Missy and Tracy signed back in at the academy, right on time, Tracy whispered, "Your brother and I loved everything we did. Of course, when we were first asked if we wanted to participate on this mission, do you know what he told me?"

Missy grinned and said, "Okaaaay. I'll bite. What did he tell you?"

"Why, he said ... and I quote ... Germany? Werewolves? Maybe some terrorists? What's not to like?"

From the Author

Thank you for reading *Tracy the Fire Witch*, my first book about Tracy but in the same world as the Missy the Werecat series. I hope you enjoyed reading about Tracy and her friends as much as I enjoyed writing about her. I've always loved stories about female characters with special powers along with stories about witches and werewolves. Future books in this series are planned, so keep checking on Amazon.

I hope you will consider leaving a review for *Tracy the Fire Witch* on Amazon, letting others know what you think about this book and this series. Word-of-mouth is crucial for any author to succeed. Your kind words, even if only a line or two, will help others decide to read about Tracy and inspire me to keep this series going for many more books. That would make all the difference and be hugely appreciated. Thanks in advance!

To be notified when P. G. Allison's next novel is released, go to: http://eepurl.com/bCtlh5 and sign up for the Missy the Werecat Newsletter. Your email address will never be shared and you may unsubscribe at any time.

Made in United States
North Haven, CT
12 June 2023

37661818R00085